Rain and Ruin

An Endless Winter Novel

By Theresa Shaver

Rain and Ruin

Print Edition

Cover Art by Melchelle Designs

Contents

Prologue

AIRIA East

"Sync complete, full diagnostic scans indicate AIRIA West is green across all boards. AIRIA West detects one hundred thirty-eight lifeforms within protective structure. One authorized level green user, Skylar Ross. Four authorized level yellow users. One hundred thirty-three level red users. Do you wish to override command now?"

"No, continue monitoring for now. We'll wait for the rain to clear before we start the evacuation to the west. Until we know the exact dynamics of the group, it's better if they don't know we're coming."

Chapter One ... Rex

The door slides closed silently behind me but it echoes in my heart like a gong of finality. I can't believe she kicked us out. I won't believe that she really meant what she said. She's broken, hurt and scared after what happened with Ted. Once she has a little time to recover and see that Ben's safe, she'll change her mind. I won't believe she doesn't feel the same way I do.

Matty and Sasha stand quietly in front of me waiting for me to lead them away but I'm just not ready yet. I turn around and place a hand against the rock façade that separates me from her and see the broken cover of the keypad hanging by one hinge. She did that for me and Matty. She risked her life and the secret of her home to save us and we brought death and danger inside with us. I take a closer look and see that the metal pin that held the hinge is bent so I take the time to bend it back into place and reattach the cover properly. It's the least I can do.

Sasha tugs at my arm but I shove her hand away. I can't talk to her yet. I don't even know who she is anymore. The girl I thought of as a sister betrayed me and put Matty in danger as well as Sky and her brother. I'll need some time to figure all that out before I can deal with her.

Once I'm satisfied the cover will stay in place, I turn and take Matty's hand and start walking. They're not far; I can hear them before we see them. The sound of axes against wood rings clear through the forest. We walk through a small patch of dead trees and there they are, all the people from the hotel. Sasha lets out a cry of relief and bolts ahead to where I see Belle and Ethan working together to set up a tent. Next to them are Lance and Marsh. They're stringing up a tarp between trees. I'm glad to see my family is safe and all together but it's dampened by the loss of Sky.

Matty runs to Belle, the only mother he's ever really known but I walk past with just a nod. She frowns in confusion but a quick glance at Sasha's shame-filled face has her looking back at me with compassion. She doesn't know the whole story but she knows what loss looks like and my face must be filled with it.

I drop the pack Skylar gave me and the med kit before I grab a corner of the tarp with my good arm to help Lance and Marsh get it secured. It won't be enough of a shelter for long but it's all we have right now against the elements.

"Rex, man, what happened? Where's that wag, Ted?" Marsh asks once the tarp's up.

I shake my head wearily and scrub at my face causing me to wince at the pressure it puts on my shoulder wound.

"Sky killed him but not before he did some damage in there."

"DUDE, you're bleeding! What happened?"

Lance's head shoots up at the concern in his son's voice and waves Ethan over to us. They help me get my jacket off and Ethan slowly peels the towel away from my shoulder. It blazes with pain as some of the blood that had dried to it rips away. Belle rushes over and has the med-kit open and is ripping packages of gauze apart to hand to Ethan. I just stand there and let them hover around me as I look back towards the entrance to Sky's home. I ignore all their questions until I hear Sasha spit out, "She threw us out!" in a nasty tone.

That has me almost snarling at her.

"And why is that, Sasha? Why did she throw us out, huh? Why did we just lose any chance of living safely and comfortably in her home? Is it because YOU betrayed us ALL?" I'm practically screaming at her and Lance has to pull me back and away before I say anything else. Her face is paper white and tears fill her eyes but I just don't care so I throw off Lance and stomp away.

Lance and Marsh follow me until I come up against a stand of trees. I'm so mad and sad and I just want to roar so I do and then I follow it up with the dumbest thing ever. I punch the tree in front of me with all I've got. The pain is so intense I drop to my knees and it takes everything inside of me not to puke. When the tears clear enough so I can see again, I look up and see Lance has a half smirk on his face.

"What?" I practically snarl at him.

He rubs a hand over his mouth like he's trying to wipe away a bigger smile from forming.

"Well Rex, you just learned a very valuable lesson that almost every boy learns on his way to being a man." At my blank look he chuckles, "Don't punch inanimate objects - it really hurts!"

I let my head drop, he's right, that was stupid and now my knuckles throb in time with my shoulder wound on the other arm. It's no relief at all from the pain in my heart.

Lance and Marsh settle down on the ground beside me and Lance puts a hand on my good shoulder.

"Tell us what happened. Marsh filled me in on what happened while I was gone on the scout and Sasha leading Ted up to this bunker but what happened after he got in?"

I let out a deep breath before I fill them both in on what happened inside with Ted and Skylar. Marsh's face is filled with anger when I explain what Sasha had done and said but Lance just listens patiently. I'm reminded again how lucky Matty and I are to have these people in our lives. Lance has been more of a father to me than my own ever was. He always listens and he's taught me so much over the years, not just how to survive but how to be a good man while doing it.

"I'm sorry, Rex. It sounds like you found more in there than just a shelter for us. This Skylar, she must be pretty special. Do you think she might change her mind?"

I shake my head wearily. "I don't know. She was pretty shaken up by what went down. Her Dad drilled her a lot about not trusting anyone outside so it was a huge step for her to make the offer in the first place. After what Sasha did and finding out that Ted was the one who killed her Dad, I just don't know if she would take another chance."

Lance glanced over towards the new camp before nodding to me. "Alright, we should be able to stay here for at least three days. We need to send out some scouts to start looking for a new shelter. Belle told us that Ted had a hunting lodge he and Mickey were headed to so we'll start looking for it or anything else we might be able to use. If Skylar hasn't changed her mind by then we'll have to move on. With the radioactive cloud just passing we should be ok out here for a while. It'll be cold and miserable but as long as we have plenty of fires we should make it until we find shelter."

I looked back in the direction of Sky's door again before letting my shoulders slump and nodded. "What about going back to town?"

Lance's expression turned grim. "Not an option. The animals from the resort were planning on moving in. We need to be very, very careful with them. They aren't men anymore. They're monsters."

Marsh and Lance helped me to my feet and I let out a groan. My knee had stiffened up while sitting on the cold ground. I now had three of four limbs in pain. I felt next to useless as we went back to the camp and started to put up more tarps and the few tents they had managed to bring with them.

The little bit of food and water people had brought with them as well as what Lance had recovered from Ted and Mickey's trailer wouldn't last very long. Lance was right, if Skylar didn't change her mind we would have to move, and soon.

Looking around at the people in the clearing was depressing. Some were working on setting up shelters and some were chopping wood but the majority were just sitting around with defeated expressions on their faces. Most of these people had been living in the hotel since the very beginning but now they were faced with the bare bones of survival. I just don't know if they will be able to adjust.

Ethan startles me out of my dark thoughts when he walks up and hands me two pills and a steaming mug of soup.

"I want you to take these, drink the soup and then go lie down. Your body's done, Rex. There's nothing you can do tonight but we'll need all hands on deck tomorrow. Get some rest."

That sounds good to me. I'm so tired and I just want to let everything go right now. I toss back the pills and sip at the soup until it's gone then hobble to one of the tents and crawl under a pile of blankets. I try and blank my mind but Skylar's heartbroken face stays front and center. I just want to fix it, fix her, but I'm so afraid she'll never give me the chance. It isn't until Matty crawls into the tent and snuggles up to my side that I finally relax enough to slide into sleep.

Chapter Two ... Skylar

Benny is a heavy weight against my side and his even breathing tells me he's finally asleep. I wish he would talk to me, tell me what he's thinking, and tell me he's ok. I don't know how to fix this, fix him. He went from never seeing another human but me and Dad so long ago to having a best friend and then a gun jammed into his neck. He saw the worst and the best of the world in three short days. So did I, but that doesn't matter. I shove aside the pain and sorrow for the moment and focus on Ben; he's all that matters now. He doesn't wake up when I lift him and carry him into his room and settle him under the covers so I back out quietly and return to the living room.

I take a good look around and see some of the damage Ted had wrought. There's broken glass on the floor and drops of blood on the carpet. My lips start to quiver when I realize that this doesn't feel like home anymore. Silent tears are running down my face as I start to pick up the glass pieces from the floor. This is me, this is how I feel, like shattered glass. I'm so sad, so alone. For a brief moment, I had thought there was a chance there would be more for my life than this cave and taking care of Benny. I thought I would have something for me, something more. A soft sob escapes as I start scrubbing the carpet where drops of Rex's blood stain it.

For the first time in a long time, I feel like a kid and all I want is my Mom and Dad. I wipe my nose with my sleeve and look up. My voice is a broken whisper when I say, "AIRIA, comfort mode on please."

Kneeling on the floor, I let my head drop and close my eyes, waiting for it. When the sound of my mom's voice floods the room, my shoulders start to shake.

"Skylar, honey? Are you OK? It's ok, honey. Everything will be fine."

"Oh, Mom, I miss you. I miss you so much! I don't know what to do! Ben, Benny's hurt and I don't know how to fix him!" My whole body is shaking with the sobs I can't hold back anymore.

"So proud of you, Sky. I love my babies so much."

I know that the words are just recordings of the things she said before she died but they're like a warm hug wrapping around me. This is only the second time I have ever let AIRIA play back her words and voice. It's just too hard hearing her again but right now I need my mom.

"I killed someone. I shot and killed a bad man who was hurting Benny. His body's still in the cavern."

This time it's my dad's voice that replies. AIRIA has a much bigger library of recordings for him.

"Skylar, you did what you had to do. Protect Ben, keep him safe, that's all that matters."

Dad's matter of fact tone helps me get control of my tears. I nod my head, that's my job, protect Benny. I wipe my face clear of tears and push myself to my feet with a shuddering breath. Ted's body needs to be removed. I can't let Benny see it again so I straighten my shoulders and palm open the cavern door. There's more work to be done.

"AIRIA, comfort mode off."

It takes me hours to drag Ted's stiff body to the incinerator that we use to burn our trash and get the blood cleaned up and to unpack the truck of the supplies we had loaded into it. My whole body and mind are numb of feelings by the time I crawl into bed beside Benny. I need to be near him before I can sleep.

My sleep is filled with the horror of scene after scene of what had happened that day. From Ben's blank face as Ted jammed the gun against his throat to the sound of the flames catching onto Ted's clothes before I slammed the metal hatch closed on the incinerator. Rex's pleading face floats between the memories as he begs me to let him stay. I wake up feeling more tired than when I had gone to sleep and covered in a clammy cold sweat. I roll over to try and go back to sleep but seeing Ben's side of the bed is empty has me bolting up and out of the bed and room. My pulse is speeding like a freight train until my eyes land on my brother. He's sitting on the couch, crashing his car against a guardrail on the TV in the video game he's playing. He glances my way and gives me a brief smile before his eyes go back to the screen.

"Morning Sky, what's for breakfast?"

I just stand staring at him for a few seconds. He seems totally fine. All traces of the blank detached kid from last night are gone. I chew on my lip in concern. Is he that resilient or has he blocked out what happened? Either way, I'm happy to have him back so I just answer him.

"How about some pancakes and fruit?"

He makes a vague yum sound so I shove my hair back and twist it into a messy bun and head to the kitchen to make breakfast. I can't keep from looking over at him every few minutes. Should I bring up what happened? Should we talk about it or should I just leave it alone? I have no idea what the best way to deal with it should be. So many times in Ben's short life, I've struggled with how to be a parent to him when so many times I've needed a parent for myself.

When the pancakes are ready, I cut and arrange strawberries in a happy face on top of them and place the plate on the kitchen island breakfast bar.

"Benny, breakfast is ready!"

I wait for a minute but he just keeps at his video game.

"BENNY!"

He jumps slightly and shoots me a guilty smile before shutting his game down and bouncing over. I wash the dishes in the sink as he plows through the meal. When he finally comes up for air, he mumbles through a mouthful of pancake, "Where's Matty and Rex?"

My hands freeze in the hot soapy water and I slowly look up into his eyes.

"They're gone, Ben."

His eyebrows shoot up in surprise like he doesn't remember what had happened the day before. He swallows what's in his mouth and takes a sip of his orange juice before asking, "Did they go to get the rest of their friends? How long until they're back? Can Matty have another sleep over?"

My mouth drops open in disbelief but I quickly snap it closed. He really has blocked out what happened. Am I going to have to explain it all to him or should I just evade and try to gloss over it? I let out a sigh and shake my head. I can't lie to him. Better he knows what happened than it surfacing later on.

"Listen, Ben, I know how much you like Matty but some really bad stuff happened because we let them in here. I can't take the risk of you getting hurt again. I'm sorry but they won't be coming back."

His little face scrunches up in confusion as he cocks his head to the side. It almost looks like he's sad for me.

"Sky, everything's ok. I'm fine and you shot that bad guy dead so you don't have to worry about him. Everything's fine now. Rex and Matty and their friends can come and live in the barracks just like you said!"

My eyes widen in shock. He remembers everything and he's ok with it? I, wow, just wow. The kid's handling things better than I am but that doesn't change anything. I won't take another chance on his safety.

"Benny, you don't understand. We can't be sure that someone else from their group won't try and take what we have or try and hurt us. I'm sorry but I'm just not willing to take that chance. No one else will be coming back inside!"

His face changes to an expression I have never seen before. It's a mix of anger and stubbornness.

"That's not fair! It was just one bad guy. You can't blame them all for him! Skylar, they need our help. I heard what Rex and you were talking about and Matty told me about how they live. We have so much stuff here and room for them all to come and live and be safe and warm and have food! It's not fair for us not to share it with them.

"Sky, Matty's my friend. I didn't even know what that really meant until we let them in. You were laughing with Rex! You were happy!"

I just stand there with the dishes forgotten and the water cooling around my hands. How can I make a boy, this seven-year-old, understand the dangers we might face if we do what he wants? I can't, so I won't.

"No Ben, they won't be coming back in. I won't go through that again!"

Ben has always been a sweet, well-behaved child in the past but he clearly has strong feelings about this issue. Even so, it's a huge shock to me when he shoves his plate off the counter and it splashes into the sink soaking me with dish water. This time, my mouth stays open in shock when he hops down from the stool and almost screams at me.

"You are the meanest person ever! And you're really selfish!"

He spins around and charges into his room but not before he slams his door as hard as he can.

All I can do is mop up the spilled water as the tears flowing down my face add to the puddles.

Chapter Three ... Rex

I wake up cold, stiff, and alone. The pale, endless winter light filters through the thin nylon tent walls giving me enough light to see that I'm alone in it. I can hear a multitude of noises from the camp that surrounds me but have no desire to join them. My first thoughts on waking are of the events from the day before and Sky's broken expression the last time I saw her face.

I keep going over and over everything that happened and what I might have done differently. It all comes down to Sasha and her betrayal, none of it would've happened if she hadn't of brought Ted in. I just can't wrap my head around why she did it. I get that she was scared for her mom but she had to know that we would have done anything to get Belle back. She didn't trust us and she let her jealousy and dislike for Sky lead her emotions. Sasha put me and Matty, her family, in danger so maybe she doesn't see us as the family I thought we were. As for Sky, there's nothing I can do but hope she changes her mind.

I slam my head back against the flat camp pillow in frustration causing all the injuries I have to flare up in pain and a groan slips out. I'm just trying to push myself up to a sitting position with my swollen hand when the tent flaps are pushed open. It's Belle that ducks in with a steaming mug in her hand. She frowns at the grimace of pain on my face and quickly sets the mug down in a clear area on the floor before helping me up.

"Rex, honey, I'm glad you're awake. How are you feeling? I brought you some herbal tea. Lance and Ethan were able to grab some of my dried herbs and some clippings from my pots before they had to evacuate the hotel so we have a small supply for tea and cooking. I also brought you some painkiller pills from the med kit you brought out with you. They should help get you more mobile. I also wanted to change the bandages on your gunshot wound. The last thing we want is for you to get an infection!"

I grab her fluttering hands as she tries to open my shirt to get at my injury. The way she's talking nonstop and acting, I know she's nervous and upset.

"Belle, stop. I'm not mad at you and I don't blame you for what happened."

Her face crumbles for a split second before it firms back up but there's a sheen of tears in her eyes.

"Rex, what Sasha did was horrible but you have to forgive her! She made a mistake out of fear. Fear for me! Please try and understand what she was feeling and try and forgive her!"

Her tears and pleading pierce my heart, she had stepped in and been mine and Matty's mother since the very first day. I love her for who she is and all that she has done for us but it isn't going to be that easy for me to get over what her daughter had done. I tighten my grip on her hands to get her to stop talking.

"Belle, I love you and I can never repay the debt I owe you for taking Matty and me in and helping to raise him. I just can't get my head around what Sasha did! She totally threw me and Matty under the bus with no hesitation. She traded the lives of four other people, two that are just kids, for what she wanted. I'd love to believe that she did it out of pure fear because I could maybe forgive that but honestly, the main reason she did it was out of jealousy! She hated Skylar on sight and was mean and petty to her. Even after what she did, Sasha still blames Sky for kicking us out. I'm sorry Belle. I don't know Sasha anymore. She's not who I thought she was and I won't ever trust her with mine and Matty's lives again."

Belle pulls her hands from mine and uses them to wipe her tear streaked face before giving a brisk nod.

"I understand how you feel Rex but Sasha's my daughter so I can't give up on her the way you can. We're a package deal and that won't ever change. She made a mistake and she'll have to live with the consequences of it but she's also still very young and we all have to take that into consideration."

She looks down and pulls open the package of gauze in her lap and starts peeling off tape to change my bandages.

There's not a lot more I can say to her on the subject of her daughter that wouldn't alienate her completely. There's no point reminding her that youth is no longer a defence in this world we live in when bad decisions could end up getting people killed.

We stay silent as she tends to my wounds and rewraps the elastic bandage around my knee until the tension in the tent is thick enough to cut with a knife. I can't take it anymore so I break the silence.

"So, where is everyone? What's happening out in the camp?"

Belle still won't meet my eyes as she gathers up the discarded packaging to burn but at least she answers me.

"Lance and Marsh left a few hours ago to do some scouting. They're trying to find a place where we can all have shelter of some sort and looking for food and water at the same time. Ethan's tending to the others from the hotel who are mainly sitting around moaning about life. At least a few of the men are trying to help by chopping wood to keep the fires going. It's been awhile since I've spent long periods outdoors but it doesn't seem to be as cold as I remember. It's still cold but it doesn't have the bite it used to."

She turns to leave the tent without looking at me but pauses at the door flap. Without turning around, she speaks to me one more time.

"When you and Matty disappeared, I almost lost my mind. I was so scared I had lost you. I'm glad you're both ok. Come out and get something to eat. There's work to be done." Then she's through the flap and gone.

I close my eyes for a minute and breathe deeply before letting it out. I have to look forward, to how we'll all survive. What's done is done and I can't go back and change it. So I'll hope Skylar will change her mind and let us all into the barracks but I can't count on it. As I push myself to my feet to leave the tent I groan at the aches that flare up throughout my body but push them aside as well, like Belle said, there's work to be done.

I shove the flaps aside and leave the tent, surprised that it's almost as dim outside as in. I glance up at the sky and frown at how dark the cloud cover is today. The sun has been a distant memory for years but this morning's sky is darker than usual. I automatically reach into my jacket pocket for the gloves I keep there to protect my hands from the stinging temperature but I'm slightly surprised that the cold isn't as bad as it normally is. Belle's right, it is warmer.

I look around the makeshift camp and see over a hundred people filling a clearing that gets bigger with every tree chopped down for firewood. Most of them are just huddled around the many fires doing nothing but looking miserable. They've been locked inside the hotel for the past seven years with only a few of them leaving to scout or scavenge. The rest don't know how to live in the real world now so they sit around and wait for someone to fix it for them. I shake my head in disgust, as it looks like that'll be Lance and the rest of our group.

I grab a quick bowl of watery soup with just a few of our hard grown vegetables floating in it and drink it down. Things are going to get really tight for us if we don't find food and water soon. Our best and only course of action might be leaving this group of strangers. There won't be enough to go around for very much longer.

I see Matty waving at me from the other side of the clearing as he follows along behind Ethan who is checking everyone's health. I have to admire the guy for staying true to his oath as a doctor and trying to help others. He's a great role model for my brother and seems to have a never-ending supply of patience when it comes to Matty's constant chatter and questions. There's no denying that Lance and Ethan have been incredible father figures to us since we met. I would do anything to protect and keep our small family safe.

This thought has me searching the camp for Sasha's telltale red hair. She missed that memo about loyalty and family. I don't see her right away but I can hear Belle's voice murmuring from one of the tents so I guess she's hiding out. That works for me, I've got nothing to say to her right now. At least nothing nice.

I use a rag to clean out my bowl and stack it back with the others before heading over to check in with my brother and Ethan. They have the medical side covered so I spend the rest of the day splitting dead wood and helping some of the people with kids to create basic lean-tos. They're pretty flimsy but it'll give them some minor protection from the elements.

I'm so relieved to see Lance and Marsh come back into camp just before dark. I'm sick of dodging questions from these people on where we're going next and where their next meal will be coming from. It doesn't seem to matter to most of them that I'm just a teenager, they just want someone to fix this mess. I stack the last log that I've split and hand over the precious ax to one of the men standing around before heading over to our tents.

My shoulder and knee are throbbing with every step. I know I over did it but sitting around nursing my injuries isn't something I feel I can do right now. All I want at this moment is to sit down with something to eat and a few pain pills but I know we have to conserve the small amount that came in the med kit for more serious injuries that might come in the future.

It feels like my stomach is kissing my spine it's so empty. It's a relief when I get closer to our tents and I can see Lance and Marsh pulling cans from their backpacks and handing them over to Belle and Matty. They found food! I try not to be bitter as they both turn and start walking to the other fires to hand out some of the food.

Marsh looks up and shoots me his trademark cocky grin before dumping the rest of his cans out on the ground. It's not a lot for so many people but it's a win that they found anything. Lance adds what's left in his pack to the pile and sorts out the cans before pulling three out and passing them to Ethan. The rest go back into his pack before he tosses it into one of the tents.

I ease myself down onto a stump by the fire and watch as Ethan opens the cans and dumps the condensed tomato soup, green beans and canned chicken into the pot over the fire. I let out a sigh when he adds a lot of water to the mix. There goes any chance of flavor. I shoot him a smile when he looks at me across the fire. Its food and we're lucky to have it. But man, the memory of Skylar's pizza isn't that far away.

Matty's back quickly and he drops to the ground in front of me and leans back against my legs. The look on his face tells me he's thinking something similar so I give his head a rub. He lost something too when Sky kicked us out. It doesn't take long before the soup's ready and everybody gets a bowl and settles down. I notice Sasha sitting somewhat outside the circle behind her mom but don't care. Lance takes a few spoonfuls of soup before looking around at all of us.

"So, Marsh and I found three small hunting cabins that were spread out over quite a distance. At the most, they could each house ten people as long as they don't mind sleeping on the floor. Tomorrow we'll go in a different direction and hope to find better." He pauses to eat some more soup and look out over the rest of the camp before he continues. "I just don't see us finding a place big enough to house everyone here. We'll have to split up into smaller groups. It sucks but the bottom line is, we are not responsible for all these people. We'll help as much as we can but we have to take care of our own as well. I think if we don't find this lodge Ted was heading to tomorrow then the following day our group and anyone who wants to follow us should head west towards Banff. It was a decent sized town so we shouldn't have a problem finding shelter and more supplies."

Ethan sets his bowl down and leans closer to the fire. "What about Canmore? We'd have to get pretty close to town to hit the highway and with those monsters there now that could get scary."

Marsh scrapes the last bean from his bowl and nods. "We don't really have a choice. The few cans of food we might find out here won't be enough. Pops, Rex and I will go scout the outskirts of town to see if they've posted any men. We also need to hit some of our caches to bulk up our supplies. It'll be a tip-toe mission but one we can't afford to not do."

Lance nods his head. "He's right, we'll need those supplies. We'll go in at dawn and leave the trailer at the edge of town. We'll make as many trips as we can before they start moving around and then hole up somewhere for the day. You guys will have to move whoever is coming with us back down closer to the highway but out of sight. As soon as it gets dark we go for the highway. We'll need to walk for quite a while before making camp. We don't want to be anywhere close to those monsters."

After everyone's done eating and the bowls are put away, Lance, Ethan and Marsh go around and talk to the other people about what they plan on doing. The pain pills Ethan made me take before dinner start to kick in so I grab Matty and head to bed. Just before I duck down into the tent I look back in the direction of Skylar's hidden door. It's about thirty kilometers from Canmore to

Banff which might as well be from here to the moon in this wrecked world. If she doesn't open that door before we leave for Banff, I will probably never see her again.

Chapter Four ... Skylar

He won't talk to me, he just glares at me and stomps away whenever I get too close. I heard him asking ARIA about the people outside and I know if he had the clearance he would open the doors no matter what I said. I wish he could understand that I'm doing this for him. My head hurts from the tension and stress of the past two days and I just want my sweet brother back.

"Hey, Benny, how about we have something special for dinner tonight? You pick, anything you want!" My fake happy tone of voice does nothing for him. All he does is scowl and turn to walk away but he stops and whirls around to face me.

"What do you think Rex and Matty are having for dinner? I'll have what they're having! You're so selfish Sky, and a coward! You're going to let all those people out there die!" he yells at me before stomping away.

I watch the angry set of his shoulders as he stomps away before closing my eyes and sighing in defeat. I'm not going to soothe this over anytime soon. I can't believe my sweet funny little seven-year-old brother can speak or even think of me this way. His words are a distant echo of what I had said to my father when I first found out all that we had for just the three of us. The kid is smart, he gets way more than I thought he did but it doesn't change anything. He's just going to have to stay mad at me. It'll be hard but at least he'll be safe.

My head is throbbing from the stress as I look in the fridge for something to make for dinner. My eyes fill with tears, again, as I think about what Rex and Matty will be eating. Uggg! Enough! I slam the door of the fridge. If Ben wants to eat, he can make his own dinner tonight! I fly into my room and grab my sneakers and quickly tie them on. I need some space and the calm that happens when I run.

The long tunnel to the barracks gets me warmed up with a light jog until I palm the door open and blast through the offices. I hit my stride as the lights come on ahead of me as I race through the huge cavern. By the second lap, my mind starts to clear and that sweet numbness closes in. All I think about is my next stride as my footsteps ring out into the emptiness. By the tenth lap, my headache is gone and I start to slow until I'm back at the start by the offices. I lean over and place my hands on my knees until I get my breath back. When I look up and out at the empty room, I finally feel calm and centered. The empty cots look back at me. I move my eyes away from them and they land on the doors to the food storage rooms. Rooms full of food that will probably never be eaten. Cots that will never be slept in. Heat and clean water that will only ever comfort me and maybe my stubborn little brother. I walk over to one of the empty cots and lie down. I'm so tired and mentally drained. I just want it all to go away.

I dream of Rex and his smile. I dream of Ben and Matty laughing like loons together as they build their cushion fort. I dream of us being a family and then it changes to cold, starving faces moving against the snow and ash that flies with the wind as the people I've come to care for try and find safety. When I finally wake the next morning I'm drenched in sweat and my body aches with tiredness even more than when I fell asleep. This is becoming a routine for me, sleep but no rest.

I wait for the tears to come again but they don't. I know what I have to do. Everything my father said was right. I can't trust anyone but me with Ben's safety but I also can't just let those people die out there. I have to find a balance. One that will keep us safe but also one that will allow me to sleep at night. Leaving them out there to die when I have all these resources not being used would make me a monster. That's not who I am and that's not what I want Ben to think of me. He needs to grow up with that balance if I want him to be a good and smart person.

I need to make a plan to make this happen so I roll off the cot to my feet before looking up at the ceiling.

"AIRIA, I need your help."

I spend the next hour going over logistics and access levels with her before I'm finally satisfied with the balance that will help those people and keep Ben and me safe. Ben's not going to be totally thrilled with my plan but at least he won't be looking at me like I'm a monster anymore. They can have all of it but no one will be allowed in our area. AIRIA will provide minimal support to keep things running in the barracks and basic questions will be answered for them, but I'm out. Benny and I will stay on our side away from them. I'm not going to be a part of anything they do over here. I'll never take another chance with Benny's safety, no matter what he says to me. They can have it all, except for one room. The armory will stay locked down with no exceptions. I won't give these people weapons that they can turn against me.

I do a last tour through all of the rooms in the barracks before diving in to get a few things prepared for their arrival. It takes me hours to get it all set up so they can get a good start in their new home. I don't even really know why I'm going to all this effort but it feels right so I just get it done and then I head back to our living quarters. Just before I leave the barracks, I take one more look back to say goodbye. I don't plan on ever coming here again. My running will go back to the treadmill.

My feet are slow as I trudge down the tunnel. I know what I'm doing is the right thing but it will be very hard to see Rex and his brother and keep my resolve of staying separate. When I step into the living room Ben's head shoots up and I see a look of relief on his face before it hardens back up. It was the first time I hadn't slept next door to him in his whole life and it hurts me to know I cause him worry. Maybe it's not such a bad thing. Maybe he'll understand a little better how I've felt since the day he was born.

I grab a shower and make some food for us, leaving his plate on the counter. I'm not going to fight with him today. I know I'm dragging my feet as I do the daily chores with the animals and garden but I'm just not ready. It's getting close to supper time when I finally start gearing up to go outside. I see Ben out of the corner of my eye watching me but say nothing. He'll know soon enough what's about to happen. I turn and look into his eyes briefly before nodding and palm open the airlock door. I don't look back and it closes behind me as I step through.

I don't give myself a chance to think about it anymore. I just grab a communicator and move to the next door. I take a deep breath and palm it open and then step out. The clearing in front of my door looks the same as the last time I was out here but the noise is different. Instead of the quiet dead forest with no sound except the wind, I hear the chop of an ax against wood and the snap and crack of more than one fire. I take the first step towards the noise and push all my emotion away.

I make my way through and around the groups of people that are huddled around campfires. The smoke from so many fires that are keeping them alive in the cold is like a haze clinging to the ground. I keep my head down and don't make eye contact with anyone. I'm not ready to talk to Rex yet. It's been three days since I exiled him, Sasha and Matty. My skin is crawling and the hair on the back of my neck is standing up while I walk through more people than I've seen in the last seven years. I feel panic start to overcome me being in the middle of so many people but push it down as I come to the end of the campfires. I take a quick look back at the way I've come but I don't see Rex or his friends. There are a few tarps and tents set up to one side so they might be in one of them. Surrounding the camp where my dead forest used to be are stumps of trees. It amazes me that they have cut down so much in just a few days.

I pick out the widest stump I can find, push back my hood, take a deep breath and step up on the stump. No one is looking my way and I'm not going to yell for attention so I pull my handgun and fire a shot into the air. There are a few startled screams and some jump to their feet but most people are too cold to move more than their heads to look my way. I see more movement as a few people dash out from the tents and tarps. There's Rex and Marsh followed by Sasha and other people I don't know. Rex's face splits into a huge grin as he sees me but I'm not out here for that so I look away and focus on the air just above the main crowd.

"My name is Skylar Ross. My home is behind you inside that mountain. Beside my home is a huge empty cavern. It has plenty of space for all of you with electricity, heat, hot water and all the food and supplies you need to live comfortably. It's yours. I don't care what you do in it or how you run it."

"There is only one condition. Your former leader, Ted, came into my home and put a gun to my seven-year-old brother's neck. He threatened us and tried to take my home from me. I killed him.

The same thing will happen to anyone who tries to gain entry into my home. You stay on your side and I'll stay on mine."

"Just in case anyone thinks they can overwhelm me, you should know that there is an A.I. computer that controls all the mechanics of the barracks and I control it. I won't hesitate for an instant to order it to cut all of the services off if I feel threatened."

No one moves and no one speaks when I pause to take a breath. My eyes glance over at Rex and I see he looks confused and hurt so I look away again.

"There are doors that will open shortly to the north of you. I suggest you gather your things and go inside them."

That's it. That's all I have to say to these people. They can figure out the rest with AIRIA's help once they're inside. I'm about to step down from the stump and get AIRIA to open the barracks doors when the alarm from the communicator blares out, followed by AIRIA's voice.

"Skylar Ross, a meteorological anomaly has been detected. Seek shelter immediately."

I look up at the sky and frown in confusion. The temperature's not dropping, if anything it actually feels a little warmer. The sky is the same boiling grey, black it's always been. I don't see or feel a problem until there's a sting on my upturned cheek. I reach my hand up to rub it away when something hits the back of my hand and it too starts to sting and then burn. I look closely at my hand but all I see is a drop of water. Then I understand, it's raining. It's raining for the first time in seven years!

I look up and out at the crowd in wonder until another drop hits my forehead and starts to burn. And that's when the screaming begins.

Chapter Five ... Rex

"I'm sorry Rex, we don't have a choice. We can't stay here anymore. We didn't find anything out there today and the little bit of food and water left will be needed to travel into Banff. I know you hoped that your friend would change her mind but it's been three days and we have to go."

Lance squeezes my shoulder to try and lessen the impact of his words but I had already resigned myself to Skylar not changing her mind so I give him an understanding nod. He pulls out the tattered map and starts to spread it out on the tent floor when a gunshot blasts out in the camp.

We all freeze for a moment before lunging for our meager weapons and out the flap of the tent. I scan around looking for the threat and freeze again when I look in the direction everyone else is. My face cracks into a smile so big my cheeks hurt. There she is, my girl, standing on a stump. I knew she wouldn't let me down! Our eyes meet for a brief moment before she turns away and starts speaking. My smile slowly melts away at her words. Our people will be safe now but what about us? How can she not feel the same way I do about her?

I can tell she's done her speech and I'm about to race through the crowd towards her when her alarm goes off and AIRIA's words boom out of the speaker at her waist. I see her flinch. She raises her hand up and then finches again before her eyes go huge and she looks right at me. Her eyes are filled with wonder for a brief moment before they fill with fear and then people are screaming and shoving each other.

I don't know what's happening until I start to feel stings on my face that turn to burns. I rub at my face but it feels like acid is dripping on me one drop at a time. I scream her name but it's lost in the other screams filling the camp. Marsh shoves me under the tarp and then takes off into the crowd. I search frantically for Matty and see him through one of the tents open flaps. He's crying in Belle's arms but I lose sight of them when more people push into the safety of the tent. I look up at the tarp above me and my mouth drops open when I see holes develop in the plastic. What the hell is going on?

I shove away a few people crowding under the tarp as I try and get back out to the camp. I have to find Sky. We need to get these people into the barracks. The flimsy tarps and tents we have won't last very long. Just as I reach the edge of the tarp and push through more people trying to find shelter, another gunshot booms out. The crowd freezes and screams stop just long enough for me to hear Sky yelling.

"Go north! The doors are open!"

The surge of people I was fighting through turns and heads away from the tarp in the direction she's pointing to. I get swept up in the crowd but manage to break free before I lose sight of Skylar. I stagger in her direction while trying to look every which way for Matty and Belle. I finally see Sasha's red hair in the crowd and then Lance with Matty over his shoulder. They're headed north in the direction Skylar had pointed to and I know Lance will make sure the rest of our group makes it to safety as soon as he can.

I spin back around and run towards where I last saw Sky and see her and Marsh scooping up two small kids each before they start running towards me. Sky's face is whiter than snow and her eyes are filled with panic and fear. Marsh is beside her, trying to hold on to the struggling toddler in his arms. The toddler is trying to reach his mom, who staggers along behind them. The woman is falling behind as she tries to carry two suitcases and run at the same time. I dodge around Marsh and Sky and grab the suitcases from the woman and scream at her to run.

My face, head and hands burn with every drop of acid rain that lands on them and all I can think about is getting us all under cover. The four of us start to catch up to the main group and my belly lurches as I realize that they've all come to a stop except for the pushing. I don't understand what the delay is. The doors into the barracks are big enough to drive a truck through, there shouldn't be a bottleneck causing this backup. I look over to Sky but her eyes are shut tight against the rain and red welts are starting to form on her beautiful face.

"SKY! Sky, what's happening? Are the doors not open?"

Her head swings my way and she opens her eyes to slits to see what's happening. She shakes her head and then jostles the child in her arms to a better position so she can grab the communicator on her belt.

"AIRA, are the doors open? Why aren't these people moving?" She screams into the box to be heard over all the noise of over a hundred frantic people.

"Skylar Ross, airlock decontamination procedures cannot commence until the outer doors are closed. Maximum occupancy of the airlock is forty people at one time."

Skylar screeches in frustration causing the kid in her arms to let out a matching wail of fear. She shouts over the screaming kid.

"AIRIA, override the decontamination process and open the inner doors! We're getting burned out here!"

"Skylar Ross, override accepted."

We stand with our heads down as bigger drops of the acid rain start to fall faster. It feels like forever until the crowd ahead of us starts to move but I know it's only a few moments. Both Marsh and Skylar are hunched over the small children in their arms, trying to protect them from the rain as they stagger forward. When the ground under our feet changes from dead grass to concrete, I let out the breath I didn't realize I was holding. I let the two heavy suitcases drop from my hands and quickly spin around and look back out into the dead forest to make sure there is no one left outside.

Skylar's heavy breathing is coming in gasps as she moves up beside me and does her own scan before turning away.

"AIRIA, scan perimeter for life signs. If nobody's out there then shut the outer doors!"

There's no response from the computer but the doors start closing so everyone must have made it in.

The soft sobs of the children's mother are muffled as she pulls the little boy from Marsh's arms and buries her face against his neck. We all just stand there catching our breath until Lance runs through the inner door and snatches Marsh into a fierce hug before his arm shoots out and pulls me into it.

“Thank God! I couldn’t find you. I thought you were still out there!”

He moves us back a step and looks us over to make sure we aren’t too damaged by the deadly rain and then nods with relief. His gaze swings over to Skylar who’s still standing in shock with a squirming toddler in her arms. Lance takes two steps towards her and plucks the kid away from her and set’s the kid on its feet before pulling her into his arms for her own hug. I can see her flinch but she just stands there with her arms at her side and her face pale and blank until he backs away.

“Skylar, my name is Lance. I’m Marsh and Rex’s dad. I can’t thank you enough for what you’ve done for my family. First rescuing Rex and Matty and then allowing us into your home. You’ve most likely saved all our lives.” When she makes no reply, Lance frowns and continues. “I also want to apologise for what helping us has cost you and your little brother. Rex has told me what you went through and I wish I could have stopped it. I’m sorry Skylar and thank you for all that you’ve done.”

I watch Sky’s face but it stays in a blank state. Only her eyes show just how much pain and turmoil she’s feeling. Her eyes dart my way before looking back at Lance and she nods.

“I have to go.”

Wait, that’s it? She’s just going to disappear again? No, no way. I won’t lose her again.

Chapter Six ... Skylar

My heart's banging in my chest from the chaos that just happened. What was supposed to be a "here, take it" moment turned into a flight from danger. I can still feel the heat from the small girl I had grabbed when her mother stumbled. She had felt like a small furnace in my arms as we rushed to get in the doors of the barracks. I can hear her sobbing coughs even muffled as she pushes her face against her mom's leg.

Lance seems like a nice enough guy but his words don't change what happened or what's going to happen. Rex is looking at me with these hopeful puppy dog eyes that I can't bear so I just nod to Lance and say,

"I have to go."

Lance nods back in understanding but as I go to step around him, Rex grabs my arm and swings me to face him.

"Sky, please, don't go. We need to talk about what happens now. We need to…talk."

His voice has so much hope in it that I have to look away before replying.

"There's nothing to talk about Rex. You know where everything is in the storage rooms. It's all yours. I need to get back to Ben and you need to get your people organised."

I won't look at him but he lets go of my arm so I slide around Lance and into the barracks. There are so many people in here milling around. More people than I've seen in seven years and even though the cavern is huge, I start to feel claustrophobic. My stomach is filled with nausea and a clammy sweat covers my skin. I try and keep my head down but it's hard to maneuver through the crowd that's bunched up at this end while looking at my feet. It's also hard not to look when I hear crying and moans of pain.

I can't help but look at the faces and hands that are covered with angry red burn welts. I know I have a few of my own that I've been trying to ignore until I can get back to the other side and a first-aid kit. I'm distracted by a sobbing woman who's being tended by a man. One of her eyes is flaming red and swollen almost closed. She must have had some of the acid rain go into it.

The man looks up from the damp rag he's using to dab at her eye in frustration and meets my look. Recognition fills his face and he takes a step towards me.

"Skylar? You're Rex's friend, right? I need clean water to help these people with their burns and any first aid kits you might have to spare."

Here's another person I don't know. My throat closes with more panic and I look around for a safe way through the crowd. It feels like they're pressing against me even though no one is. The man must see the panic in my eyes because he steps right up to me and takes me by both arms.

"Whoa! Take a breath, it's ok. Just breathe. My name is Ethan and I'm a doctor. I'm also Marsh's Dad. It's ok Skylar, you're safe."

I'm looking into his eyes and the kindness and compassion there calms me enough to take a steadying breath. The panic is still there but I'm getting control of it. He rubs my arms and nods encouragingly.

"Ok, can you tell me where I can find supplies to help all these people? Even clean water will help flush some of the chemicals off that caused the burns."

I swallow down the lump in my throat but my voice still comes out a croak.

"There's a fully stocked infirmary. It should have anything you need. It's over…"

I go to point the direction, but there are too many people between us and the direction he needs to go so I just shake my head.

"Follow me. I'll take you there."

I don't check to see if he's following, I just wind my way through the crowd until I break free of it and finally can take a deep breath. The infirmary is at the far end of the cavern down by the offices and the door to get me out of the barracks. I'll be able to just show him the way and then slip away to the tunnel. I need to get out of here and back to my own side before Rex tries to convince me to stay.

Ethan catches up to me and matches me stride for stride as I move away from the cots and closer to the far wall. I can tell he's looking at me but I keep my gaze straight ahead, even when he starts talking to me.

"I really can't tell you how grateful we all are that you opened up your home to us. I know things were bad with Ted and that Sasha had a hand in that but I hope you can forgive us. None of us would have deliberately caused you or your brother harm or pain. We've all seen enough misery to last a lifetime since the bombs dropped. We just want a chance to be safe and survive as best we can. You've given us all an incredible gift, Skylar."

I still have nothing to say. I hear his words and understand where both him and Lance are coming from but it'll be a long time before I get the image of a gun pressing into my baby brother's neck out of my mind. I'm glad these people will be safe now, especially after the acid rain hit but I still don't want anything to do with them. I've done all I'm willing to do, Ben has to come first.

We walk a few more paces in silence until Ethan realises I'm not going to reply and he lets out a sigh before changing the subject.

"So, this A.I.? It's a computer that runs the place? Is there anything we should know about it or how to use it?"

I feel my shoulders slump slightly as I realise that I'm not going to get away as quick as I had thought I would. When I furrow my brow in a frown, there's a burning pain on my forehead that makes me wince and raise my hand up to gently press my fingers against where the pain is. I keep walking as I move my fingers lightly over my whole face and take a count of all the small burns on it. I count six spots by the time we reach the infirmary doors. There goes my chance at winning any beauty pageants.

I palm open the double doors and use my boot to knock down the stoppers to keep them open. The lights come on the minute I open the doors. As I turn to address Ethan, I see him standing there with this look of amazed hope in his eyes that are welling up with tears. He blinks them back and looks at me with a sheepish grin.

"Sorry, I just never thought I would be in a real functioning medical unit again. You have no idea how hard and frustrating it is to be a doctor and not be able to help people properly when all you have is makeshift medicine and rags to work with. Coming in here is like waking up from a medical nightmare!"

I turn and look into the room and see it with new eyes. I feel a wash of shame as I think of all the people this room could have helped instead of staying dark and empty. I shake my head and push the shame away. There's no changing the past. We just need to make the best of what we have today. I look at Ethan again and square my shoulders.

"AIRIA, the computers name is AIRIA. She controls all the functions in here and will keep everything running. Would you say you and Lance will be taking control and organising your group?"

Ethan glances back over his shoulder to where the group is still milling about in the far end of the cavern before looking back and answering me.

"Well, we have since we left the hotel so probably."

"Ok, I'm going to give you, Lance and Rex a yellow authorization. That means you can ask AIRIA questions and for help and she will talk to you. You will be able to control the locks on the storage room doors as well but you won't be able to open the door between the barracks and my living area. If you need to get out the exterior doors you can open them too. If you really need help she can't provide, you can have AIRIA send me a message, but I'd rather your group keeps to itself." I rub at one of the worst burns on my forehead before continuing. "Rex knows where most everything is but I've locked the armory down completely. I'm not comfortable letting your group have the weapons stored in here."

As I'm talking, Ethan is nodding as he walks further into the infirmary and starts opening cabinet doors. I'm ready to just take off when he turns with a tube in his hand and beckons me forward. I look at him warily but he just laughs.

"It's just some burn cream. It'll help soothe those welts and help them heal." When I still just stand there his smile turns sad. "When was the last time someone took care of you, Skylar?"

His tone is so sympathetic that I feel tears spring up but quickly blink them away. It's my job to take care of Ben and that's all that matters. I shake my head at him.

"Yeah, um, thanks but I have my own medical supplies. You should get your own people looked after. I've got to get back to my brother so, um, good luck."

I spin away and out the door before he has a chance to say anything else and make for the offices. It's hard for me to keep my resolve strong when Ethan, Lance, and Rex are all being so nice. I know in my heart that most of these people would be kind to Ben and me but it's just the possibility that one of them won't that means it's not a chance I'm willing to take. I took a chance before and it almost got us killed. I'm almost at the doors to the office when a small voice stops me in my tracks and I squeeze my eyes shut in frustration before turning around.

"Skylar?"

I look into his sweet green eyes and see how happy he is to see me and want to cry but instead just say,

"Hi, Matty. You doing ok?"

The kid is just too cute when his grin broadens, causing his dimples to be on full display and I have no choice but to catch him when he throws himself at me for a hug. I have to keep reminding myself that Ben's safety comes before his happiness because I know what's coming next.

"Can I come with you to see Ben? Or can he come over here so he can meet the rest of my family?"

My mouth goes dry and my throat closes as I try and think of a way to explain to this little angel why that will never happen again. He's looking up at me with all the trust I can't give back when I'm saved from answering.

"Matty-man! Rex is looking for you. Scamper, pest, big bro's getting worried!"

Matty nods at Marsh but throws his small arms around me one more time before running back towards the crowd with a yell over his shoulder.

"Tell Ben I'll see him later!"

I just stand there with my shoulders slumped watching as he's swallowed up by the crowd. Marsh's words jolt me out of my funk.

"Don't sweat it Sky. You did a huge thing by letting us all in here. Now you gotta do what you think is best for you and your little man. Sometimes the best thing to do hurts the most. Just know that Rex, and me, well, we'd both lay down our lives for you and Ben. You saved us and Rex and Matty more than once now so we've got your back. No matter what you decide."

The deep breath I try and take hitches in my chest so I turn away from him so he can't see the pain I know is all over my face.

"Thanks, Marsh. That means a lot but I just…"

I feel his hand on my shoulder and it gives a brief squeeze before dropping away.

"I get it, its ok. Go on back to Benny-boy. You did good today."

The tears are starting to fall down my face and there's no way to stop them so I bolt to the doors and just keep going.

Chapter Seven ... Rex

“Matty, there you are! I’ve been looking everywhere for you.”

I snatch the kid up and give him a fierce hug before dropping him back to his feet. I keep one hand on top of his head to keep him with me as I scan the crowd looking for Sky. I don’t believe she’d take off without talking to me first but Matty’s words dash that notion.

“I was just saying goodbye to Sky. Can we go over and see Ben later?”

I close my eyes in disbelief. She really left? Man, every time I think I know what she’s thinking, I’m wrong. I shake my head and put it aside for now. There’s work to be done.

Lance climbs up on top of one of the bunks and lets out a piercing whistle causing the crowd to all go silent and turn in his direction. Once he sees everyone looking his way he starts giving directions.

“The doctor’s pretty sure that was acid rain falling out there and suggests we all make use of the showers to get the chemicals off of our skin and hair. He has burn cream to treat the burns after we shower. Before we do that, we should get a quick organization done. We’ll need some volunteers. We need a few people to help out the doctor to get everyone treated that needs it. I’m told that there are fresh clean clothes and towels in storage, so ten people please head over to where Marsh is standing and he’ll show you where that is. You guys carry it back over to the showers so everyone going in can grab fresh garb.

"Next up is food. There is a large amount available and a huge kitchen to prepare it in. Anyone who loves to cook would be welcome to help. The more we work together the faster we can get fed!

"Once we are clean and have eaten, we can look at setting up living areas. These bunks look like they can be moved so we shouldn’t have any problem putting together some separate living areas to give us all our own space. We can use the extra blankets as screens for even more privacy.

"I think that's all we should worry about today. We can have a meeting tomorrow to decide how to go forward." Lance looks at all the faces staring up at him but when no one speaks he nods. "Alright, give us a few minutes to get the supplies and you can all start lining up at the showers. Ladies showers are over there and men's are that way." He points in the two directions and then hops down from the bunk.

I walk Matty over to where Marsh is to help carry over towels and clean clothes. It's only been a few days since I had showered in Skylar's bathroom but the amazing memory of it has me eager to help everyone else feel the same. The last time I was in here the shelves were bare so Sky must have opened a few of the storage containers and pulled out what she thought we would need to get started. A bunch of people come over to help so it doesn't take long for us to start handing stacks of shrink-wrapped towels and clothing sets out. There are thick plastic bags filled with soaps and shampoos that we use to fill dispensers in both washrooms and soon there are clouds of scented steam floating out of the shower doors every time they're opened.

As I pass the long line up of women waiting for their turn, I come to a stop and shake my head before heading over to Lance.

"Hey, I don't know why I didn't think about it before but there's like ten shower rooms in here. They don't need to line up at just these two."

Lance's eyes widen in surprise and he shakes his head with a grin.

"That's good to know. We're going to have to have a tour of this place later on. I think it would be wise to know exactly what all we have to work with. Let's plan on that after everyone's settled in for the night. Now, let's go stock up a few more of the shower rooms and get these people cleaned up!"

Once Marsh and I and the others finish passing out shower supplies, he and I head out to look for Matty so we can have our own showers. We finally find him in the huge kitchen, where the most incredible smells are filling the air. He's sitting on one of the stainless steel counters kicking his feet and chewing on what looks like a granola bar. Beside him on the counter are at least thirty serving jugs filled with ice and some kind of orange drink. Belle is next, standing at a sink filling up the last few empty jugs and giving each one a stir.

I look around the rest of the kitchen and see five of the biggest pots I've ever seen gently steaming on the stoves.

"Wow Belle, I can believe how fast you guys are! How did you put this together so quickly?"

Bell sets the last jug on the counter with the others and turns to look at me with a frown.

"We didn't. It was already made." At our blank looks, she glances down to another counter where Sasha stands with a sulky face before looking back at us and explaining. "Five pots of chili. All we had to do was turn the stove on. There was also over a hundred bread rolls rising and ready to be baked. Do you know how long that would have taken to prepare? Even if it was all premixed? Your friend Skylar did this. She made this meal for you and all of us. She's a very special person Rex. I'm so very sorry."

Skylar, Sky did this. She made this meal to welcome us and comfort us. Again she makes my head spin. I just want to sit somewhere quiet with her and talk. I know if I had that chance I could get her to change her mind.

Almost like he's reading my mind, Marsh gives me a nudge.

"Hey man, you just need to give her some time and space to work it out. Think about it. She's already getting there. She's already changed her mind about letting us in here and after seeing all this I'm almost positive she'll come around. Sky's epic, she'll get there!"

His words make sense and I feel a little better but it washes away when I see that Sasha's come closer to hear what we're talking about and she has an ugly sneer on her face. It takes all I've got not to slap the look off of her face and instead I pour my contempt into my voice.

"You stupid…CHILD! She saved mine and Matty's life and probably yours too and you stand there with that look on your face? What the HELL is wrong with you? I didn't know you were so malicious and filled with jealousy. I do know that I don't want you anywhere near me or Matty!"

Her face loses the ugly expression and goes pale with shock before turning to her mother for assurance but Belle's lips are pressed tightly together in anger.

"Sasha! Go, go help set up tables. We'll discuss your attitude later!"

Sasha practically runs from the kitchen but not before I see the tears in her eyes. For a half second, I feel guilt at treating someone who's been a sister to me and Matty that way but it quickly passes. It's not just about Sky. Sasha threw both me and Matty under the bus with Ted and that's what I don't think I can forgive. As far as I can tell, she still doesn't think she's done anything wrong.

"Why is Sasha being so mean? Is she mad at us Rex?"

Oh man, how am I supposed to explain something I don't even understand to the kid? Thankfully, Belle steps in to take the hit.

"No baby! Sasha's just really confused right now and it's making her act not like herself. She loves you and Rex very much. It's just, being fifteen is a very difficult time for a girl. They go through so many changes in their bodies and minds that sometimes they do things before thinking them through. Don't worry about it, I'll be helping Sasha make better choices in the future."

"Now, you need to help out with dinner set up. Go and take a stack of those plastic cups out to the tables please."

I help Matty down from the counter and he gives Belle a funny little salute before doing as she said. As soon as he's out the door, Belle turns back to me.

"Listen, I'm not making excuses for what my daughter did but what I said to Matty is true. Sasha's hormones are all over the place right now and I know you know she had a very large crush on you, Rex. Now that I've seen Skylar, I can see where the jealousy came from. That girl is stunning! Try and think about it from Sasha's position. She thinks she's in love with you but you don't feel the same and then you find this gorgeous girl you fall for almost right away. Skylar is and has everything Sasha doesn't. She's like a dream girl with beauty and a magic wand that she waves to make everything better for everyone. Top that with Skylar being kind and generous and Sasha can't compete in any way. She's had all of us to herself for the last seven years and now she has to share? Sasha just doesn't understand that it's not a competition. She doesn't understand that we're her family and that's not going to change. Add in hormones and you've got a perfect storm!"

Belle makes a lot of sense but even with all that it's going to be hard to see Sasha the way I use to.

"Rex, what Marsh said was true. Skylar will need some time to work through all that happened but so will your sister. No matter what she thinks she feels or what she did, Sasha is your sister. I'll be helping her work through it, ok? Just give her a chance and you'll see."

There wasn't a lot I can say in response to Belle's plea so I just nod and pull her into a hug. I can't help but feel grateful to have her and the other adults in our lives to help us navigate through all our problems and feelings. It just makes my heart hurt for Skylar even more. She's been alone for so long, trying to figure out life and parenthood with no guidance except for an unfeeling computer. I hope she can find her way back to me.

Chapter Eight ... Skylar

The door slides shut behind me and I take my first real deep breath since I left to go outside. I slump back against the cool metal and take a minute to process everything that just happened while using just my fingertips to touch the few stinging burns on my face.

I try not to think about what would have happened to all those people if I hadn't let them into the barracks or even if I had waited any longer to do it. I don't know what to think about the rain coming down after so many years. Does this mean that the earth is now trying to cleanse itself or is it just more misery like the snow and ash? I'll have to ask AIRIA to let me know if anything else changes out there because I don't plan on stepping out those doors again for a long time.

I push away from the door and slowly start walking down the concrete tunnel.

"AIRIA, the doors I just came through can only be opened by me, right?"

"Skylar Ross, authorization green is needed to open the barrack doors. You are the only person with a green authorization."

"Ok, good. Did you voiceprint the two men I talked to? Lance and Ethan? I don't know their last names."

"Skylar Ross, voiceprint complete on both males with names Ethan and Lance. Authorization level for both males set at red."

"AIRIA, you can change both of their access levels to yellow and add Rex Larson to that too. They will need to ask you questions about where stuff is stored and any other things you can help them with as long as it isn't about security. Let them know what you can help them with. Oh! And you could tell them that they can ask about any of the educational stuff you helped me with too, like setting up the grow room and that they can use the computers in the offices to watch videos and also..."

I come to a stop half way down the tunnel and close my eyes. I **am** a coward! One decent conversation with them and I could have told them all of this. I could have given them a quick tour and explained everything that AIRIA could help them learn. Instead, I just ran away like a scared little girl! I know why I did it. Rex. If I had spent any time with Rex all my resolve would have crumbled. It was hard enough just talking to Matty.

"AIRIA, just, I don't know. Give them a tutorial or something!"

My feet start moving again and I give my head a shake. Like Marsh said, sometimes the best thing to do hurts the most and that's very true because more than anything right now, I want to run right back into the barracks and find Rex. I want to sit and talk with him and I want to bring him and Matty back with me and make us all dinner and…so much more. I push that thought away with the image of Ben's empty face when Ted had held the gun against his neck. Not having a future with Rex hurts but a life without Ben would kill me.

By the time I make it back to our living quarters, my resolve and barriers are as strong as the rock that surrounds us. I know what's going to hit me on the other side of the door so I'm ready when I step through.

Ben's not on the couch like I thought he would be. Instead, I see him pacing back and forth with a worried look on his face. When he sees me it clears to a giant smile before clouding back over.

"SKY! What happened to your face? AIRIA said you brought everyone inside the barracks. Did they hurt you?"

My hand automatically reaches up to touch at the burns but I quickly drop it.

"No, no, no Ben! It was - there was rain. Bad rain full of chemicals started to fall outside and a few drops hit me but it's ok! It's not as bad as it looks."

The air whooshes out of him in relief and he's back to smiling.

"Are Matty and Rex ok? Are they coming over? I'm so happy you changed your mind Sky! Can we have another pizza party sleepover soon? I'm sorry I was so mean to you!"

He doesn't give me a chance to respond because he's throwing himself into my arms and burrowing his head against me in the same spot another child did as I carried her to safety. I'm back to being his hero and awesome sister but I know it's not going to last so I just hold him tight against me and enjoy his love as long as I can. When he finally starts to wiggle I set him down and take him by the shoulders.

"Ben, do you know how much I love you? Do you know what I would do to protect you?"

His little face lights up and he nods.

"Good, it's important that you understand that everything I do is to keep you safe. You were only half right in all those things you said to me. It was the right thing to do to let all those people into the barracks. They would have died out there and we have so much here that can help them. They'll be safe now and have lots of food and water and heat and shelter to give them a better life. But, that doesn't mean that they are safe for us! We know a couple of people in that group but there are over a hundred we don't know. I will NOT ever put you in danger again or take a chance on it happening again.

"They will stay on their side and we will stay on ours. You can be mad at me if you want and you can not talk to me if you want, BUT you will NOT say mean things to me like you did last time! It's my job to keep you safe and I will do it no matter what you think. When you're older, you'll understand. Until then, we go back to the way it was before. Schoolwork, chores and some fun but it's just going to be us."

His face is full of thunder and he opens his mouth to say something but changes his mind and clamps it shut before pulling away from my hands and turning away. I watch him walk to his room and quietly shut his door. Ok then, that's that. It might take some time but one day we'll get back to normal. I hope.

I'm exhausted and my face is starting to really hurt so I head to the bathroom to take a shower and wash away the stressful day. What I see in the bathroom mirror makes me wince. I have six bright red welts that look almost like blisters on my face. The biggest one is on the side of my forehead and it hurts the most. I lean closer to get a better look and go to push my hair away from my face but the hair keeps coming out in my hand. I'm stunned as I reach up and run my hands through my hair a few more times causing even more of the strands to break away. Not only had the acid rain burnt my face but it had burnt through some of my hair too. Most of the damage is on the very front because I had flipped my hood up just after it had started raining. Looks like I'm going to have bangs.

The shower soothes the burns slightly but the burn cream I apply helps the most. By the time I'm done playing hairdresser and cutting the damaged hair away I'm completely wiped out. I quietly walk past Ben's closed door and blow it a kiss good night. He might be mad at me, but he's safe and that's enough for me right now.

Chapter Nine ... Rex

I'm helping Marsh set up tables for dinner when the computer voice of AIRIA comes out of the ceiling causing a few screams of surprise and lots of jumps from the people around me.

"Rex Larson, Ethan unknown last name, Lance unknown last name authorization increased from red to yellow. Would you like a tutorial on my functions now?"

I know right away that Sky's changed our authorization levels but I don't think we should have this conversation with AIRIA's voice booming out across the whole cavern.

"AIRIA, give us a few minutes to get together and we'll get back to you for that tutorial."

"Rex Larson, standing by."

Marsh waves me off so I go looking for Ethan and Lance. I head straight to the medical clinic knowing that it would take a crowbar to pull Ethan away from there right now. The guy's like a kid in a candy store with all those clean shiny cupboards filled with medicine magic. As I round the last set of bunks at that end of the cavern I see Lance heading that way too. I wait outside the door for him to catch up and we go in together. As soon as the doors open we hear AIRIA through the speakers set in the ceiling. She's talking about different types of antibiotics and where they are stored and how to prepare them from the current powdered state they are in. Obviously, Ethan didn't waste any time getting his tutorial.

We stand there listening for a few minutes before Lance finally breaks in.

"Ethan, can you hold on with the medical stuff for a minute?"

Ethan swings around from the counter where he had been taking notes in surprise. He hadn't even heard us come in.

"Oh, yes, of course. Uhh, computer stop."

Lance looks at me with a raised eyebrow as if to say "What now?" so I just shrug and start talking.

"Uh, AIRIA, can you not share everything we talk about with the whole cavern please?"

"Rex Larson, I will contain all responses to your queries to whatever section of the barracks you are in. Unfortunately, the acoustics of the main cavern will carry our communications quite a distance. I would suggest for privacy you only address your questions to me in one of the enclosed spaces such as this clinic or the offices where I can limit my responses to the speakers in those areas."

Lance nods and asks me, "Can you ask it about that yellow level thing and what it means?"

Before I can explain that he can ask himself, AIRIA does.

"Lance last name unknown, you may address me yourself. The three of you in this room have been given a yellow authorization level. Do you wish the full range of authorizations that entails or just the basics? Skylar Ross has told me that all details are not always needed at all times. She prefers just the basics most of the time."

I can't help but smile at that. I can almost hear Skylar saying "Just the basics AIRIA," in an impatient tone.

Lance looks at both of us again before finally addressing the ceiling.

"AIRIA, first thing, my last name is Malone and Ethan's last name is Gains. Second, just the basics, for now, will be fine."

"Lance Malone, yellow authorization allows you to address me with questions and I will respond to the best of my abilities. I will not respond to the others without authorization from yellow or higher. You can control the locks of all rooms except the armory and the main doors to the secondary cavern. Those require a green authorization level to open.

Educational tutorials are available on a wide variety of subjects as well as video archives that can be viewed on computers in the office area or on a projector that is in storage. That's the basics. An in-depth tutorial is available at your convenience. Feel free to ask any other questions at any time. I am at your disposal."

Lance has a thoughtful look on his face and nods. "Thank you AIRIA. That's all for now." He looks over at Ethan, "Can you pull yourself away from here for a bit? I'd like to go take a look at these offices and I think the food will be ready pretty soon."

I can't help but laugh when Ethan slowly nods his head as he looks longingly over his shoulder at the open cupboard doors. At least I'll know where to find him for the next month or year.

I take them over to the offices and we poke around and turn on a few screens before we find a door that leads into a set of rooms behind the offices. There are five suites that must be for the officers because they are way nicer than the main barracks. Each suite has a bedroom with a queen size bed and a living area with a kitchenette and its own bathroom with tub and shower. Right away Lance claims these rooms as ours. I have to admit, it'll be nice to have some privacy from the main group. We don't really know any of them that well and except for the few days in the hotel, we've been on our own for seven years. It's Ethan who voices a concern over it.

"Lance, don't you think the others will be upset if we take the best picks for ourselves? I don't really want a war starting in this place."

Lance shakes his head. "Honestly, I don't really care what they think. We aren't even responsible for those people. We did the right thing by getting them out of the hotel and town but it was their decision to stay under Ted's thumb all these years. If Skylar hadn't let us in here, we would have most likely left that group altogether. Don't get me wrong, I'm happy they're in here and safe but I have no interest in babysitting them all. We will have to work together and try and make some kind of society but we will continue to look after our group first." He looks over at me. "Rex, what do you think? You're the reason we're here. Skylar let us in because of you and Matty and she gave us the higher authorization because she trusts us a fraction more than the others. Do you think we should take these suites for our group or have some kind of lottery for them?"

I think about it for a moment but I honestly don't know what the right answer is. I know there has to be some sort of balance or the other group will eventually start looking at us with jealousy and I've already seen what that can lead to.

"Well, there's about twenty offices out there that we don't really need so I say we take these for ourselves and then keep two offices for organization work. The rest we empty out of desks and put bunks into. They can be for family units. If there are more families than offices we can do a lottery with some kind of rotation. As for us keeping these to ourselves, well, Lance is right. Nobody would be in here if Skylar hadn't trusted me, so for now, they're ours."

Both Ethan and Lance nod before Lance says, "Good, let's go eat!"

As soon as we came close to the tables, the intoxicating smell of fresh baked bread hit us and we all groaned in appreciation.

"Wow, that's impressive. How did they make bread so fast?" Ethan asked.

I have to grin, "They didn't. Skylar made it all before she let us in. They just had to warm it and bake it."

Ethan shook his head and said with a sad tone, "That girl has a complex." At my confused looks, he explained. "She's all about taking care of others but she won't let anyone take care of her. That's not good. One of these days, it'll break her."

As we walk the rest of the way to the tables that are starting to fill up with hungry refugees I think about Ethan's words. I think he's right and I think that she's already starting to break. I just wonder what it'll take to finish it and if she'll be able to come back if she does.

There's not a lot of talk at the tables as over a hundred people eat the first real hot meal in a very long time. The buns are snatched up quickly and I'm thrilled when Belle quietly informs us that she secreted a few away for our group to have later. But then I remember just how many supplies fill the containers in the storage area and tell her that we can have bread every day if we want.

It's a great meal but it would be even better if Sky and Ben could be here with us. I think they would love to see how their generosity made so many people happy. I'm relieved when a new group of people offers to do the meal clean up so that we can show Belle and the others our new suites. Matty runs from room to room bouncing on each bed before declaring the bounciest ours and Belle is clapping her hands in delight when she opens a closet and finds an apartment sized washer and dryer. Marsh checks every living room for a gaming system but comes up empty and jokingly starts plotting on how to dig his way to Skylar's area so he can steal hers. Sasha just follows her Mom around with a sulky face until she closes herself into what will be her and Belle's room.

It's been a long day full of extremes and I'm ready to crash but first I follow Belle and Matty to one of the storage rooms and let them in so we can get bathroom supplies. None of the other group has moved any of the bunks yet. They've all just spread out and laid down for the night. I notice as more people lay down that the lights above them dim and marvel at the computer running this place. As we head back to our rooms with our arms full of supplies, I'm not at all surprised to see Ethan going into the medical clinic, even after the long day.

I'm sure tomorrow will be another full day but hopefully not as dramatic as today was. Belle gives Matty a shower as I make up our bed with the shrink wrapped bedding. Once he's snuggled in I finally get my own shower before crawling in with him. As a gentle warmth blows down on us from the register in the ceiling, my last thought before I fall asleep is Skylar's face.

Chapter Ten ... Skylar

Ben and I spend the day not speaking to each other and by noon I've got a pounding headache. I leave him be, there's no point forcing him on anything. It's just going to take time. Instead, I put in some work on my neglected garden. It's been over a week since I dedicated any real time to it. It still astounds me how there can be weeds to pull in such an isolated garden but AIRIA has told me that they come from the soil I add every so often from the bags in the storage room. They're a real pain, but it makes me happy to know that they're growing somewhere in such a dead world. I lose myself in the mindless task and try not to think about Ben, Rex or anything else that I've had to deal with in the last while. I daydream about the day I can take my garden and transplant it outside. One day the skies will clear and the sun will shine down and heal the land. Things will grow again and people and animals will be safe to enjoy the fresh air and the kiss of the sun.

As I pick fruit and vegetables and trim away dead stems and leaves my mind starts cataloging all the shoots I could safely take away to replant in the other empty grow rooms in the barracks. I catch myself when I start thinking about how nice it will be for all of them to have fresh food again. I throw down my small trowel in frustration. They have all the seeds over there they need to start up their garden. They don't need my shoots even if it means it takes longer for them to have a harvest.

Frack, I'm weak! Yes, it was right to let them in over there but that doesn't mean it's safe to start mingling with them. Why am I so hung up on Rex anyways? I just met the guy! Yes he's very good looking and yes we have a lot in common with us both having to raise our younger siblings but that doesn't mean that the guy's my soul mate. For frack's sake! Am I that lonely and desperate that the first guy to come along with dimples can sweep me off my feet? Ok, the green eyes didn't hurt and the sweet way he looks after his brother and…Argggg!

I need to get him out of my head. I wish the last week had never happened. Ben and I could have just gone on business as usual until the day AIRIA told us it was safe to go outside. I'd really like to believe that we would have been happier that way but I can't force myself not to remember how sad Ben was when he asked about other boys and nerf gun battles. He's just as lonely as me. I also force myself to remember all the times I'd go sit outside on the hunting platform and imagine in detail another life where I'm surrounded with other people my age. That's not normal or healthy but it's what I've got.

I try and picture myself in another ten years after Ben's the age I am now. Can I do it? Can I just stay locked away and isolated until then? Can I carry on where my father left off? Filling his head as he grows with "Don't trust anyone. Don't help anyone." I know that's not what I want for him but do I have a choice? I see his tiny face the day he was born as our mother dies beside us because of what men had done to the world. I see his small face asking where his Daddy is after I've just had to bury his body from being shot in the back by another man. And then there's the look on his face as a man presses a gun against his little neck. No, I don't want this life for him but it's all we've got. We have to stay separated from others. We have to stay here alone, where we're safe.

I clean up the mess I've made in the garden and put away my tools before heading to the kitchen to make dinner. All the stress of my internal battle is making me feel sick so I need to get something to eat and clear my mind. As I walk through the door I find out that we aren't as safe alone in here as I thought because I've once again brought danger into our home.

"Sky, I don't feel very good."

Ben's standing in his bedroom doorway and he's kind of swaying. Confused, I take a few steps toward him and see how pale he is. His eyes are red-rimmed and he has two bright red spots on his pale cheeks. I've never seen Benny like this before except for one time when he was a baby and getting a new tooth. Dad said it was normal for babies to have…Oh My God! A fever! Benny has a fever. How, what does that mean? I try and think why he would have a fever but don't get very far because he rasps out a rough cough and then drops to the floor.

I'm across the room and down next to him in a half second and lift him into my arms. His skin is on fire and his head hangs lose on his fragile neck. I get him up and into bed while I'm trying frantically to figure out how or what had made him sick until it blasts through my head like a scream in my ear.

"AIRIA, override the decontamination process and open the inner doors! We're getting burnt out here!"

The little girl I had carried in had been hot too. She had been sobbing out coughs against my jacket the whole time and I didn't decontaminate after. I had just walked right in and Benny had hugged me with his face in the same spot she had left all those germs. This is my fault. For the second time, I went against everything my father had warned me about and now for the second time, Benny is in danger.

My stomach heaves and threatens to let loose at the idea of my baby being sick enough to die. He has no immune system! How can he fight off whatever this is when he's never even had a cold? I race to the bathroom and get a wet wash cloth for his head. I know I need to cool him down but what else?

"AIRIA! Benny's sick, what do I do?"

"Skylar Ross, Benjamin Ross's body temperature is elevated to a mildly dangerous level. If his temperature rises any higher, his major organs will become at risk for damage and then they will begin to shut down. Give Benjamin Ross a dose of a fever reducer such as Tylenol or Advil. Dose by weight."

My legs are trembling under me as I stagger back to the bathroom to find the pills but I don't know what dose by weight means. Benny's weight? I don't know how much he weighs. I've never had any reason to weigh the kid. I'm rushing back to his room with the pill bottle in my hand trying to read what the dosage is on the back but my eyes are blurring the words and I can't focus properly. As I try and go into Ben's room my shoulder clips the door frame sending me crashing to the floor. I lay there for a minute trying to catch my breath but end up coughing instead. That's when I know Ben's not the only one who's sick. I try and push myself up but my head is dizzy and I have to lay back down or risk falling again.

I let the tears fall down my face and onto the carpet. All my agonizing means nothing now. I have no choice but to let the people I risked everything for come back in for the third time. Hopefully this time it will be to save us instead of harm us. My voice is barely a whisper but I know she'll hear me.

"AIRIA, increase Rex Larson's authorization to green. Tell him to bring the doctor."

As my vision starts to dim my brain can't process what she says next.

"Skylar Ross, outer perimeter breach detected."

I try and say more but blackness closes in and I let my head slump to the floor.

Chapter Eleven … Rex

I'm tired but it's a good satisfied tired. We got so much accomplished today. Ethan spent the morning treating the minor burns from the rain and ailments of the large group and has plans to set up vaccinations for all the children in the barracks. I've never seen him so happy as when he found out about the stockpiles of stored medicines available to us. Belle bounced between getting the kitchen stocked up with supplies from storage to organising a team of people to start filling the garden beds and pots with bags of soil to start planting seeds. Lance, Marsh and I worked on hauling out desks and office furniture so we could fill the empty rooms with bunks for families.

Everyone from the hotel seems revived by the comforts of being in a safe place with heat, hot water, and good food. They all dove in, getting bunks moved around into separate living spaces and supplies distributed. None of our group had really gotten to know anyone from the hotel with the threat of Ted and his men hanging over us but now we were finally learning names and what skills everyone has.

Lance has plans to get a census started with everyone's skills listed and then make a schedule for different areas of work. At first, I was worried that the people would resent us for taking charge but it seems they're all happy to be doing something positive after barely surviving and cowering in fear at the hotel. I ask Lance the question that I've been worrying about since we all came inside.

"Are all of these people safe?"

Lance looks down the barracks at the people milling around and gives a thoughtful frown before answering.

"The short answer to that is, I honestly don't know. We don't really know any of these people. We weren't at the hotel long enough to interact with them much and I can't say I'm really impressed by how they all let Ted control them. I can see how the fear of everything that happened, in the beginning, could make them all follow a strong leader, but seven years of his abuse?" He shakes his head dismissively. "That's pretty weak. All I can say based on that is I don't really see any of them being a threat. Especially if our group keeps control of things. Most of them will just follow along with what we suggest and be thankful we aren't cruel like Ted and his men."

I nod in agreement to that but I'm still concerned that we may have brought a threat in with us.

"What about Ted's men? What happened to all of them?"

Lance's face turns grim. "Not a lot of them made it back from the group he sent with me to scout the ski resort. They either didn't survive the radiation cloud or the savages picked them up. When I made it back to the hotel, it was in chaos. People had found out that he and Mickey had taken off with most of the supplies and the water had stopped flowing. There were only five of his guys left there and I saw three of them take off with backpacks in the opposite direction than us. The other two decided to come with us but I…persuaded them not too. They disagreed so I had to permanently persuade them. I wasn't going to have them with us as a constant danger so I did what I had to."

He looks over at me to see my reaction so I just nod that I agree with what he had to do. He pushes off from the wall we're leaning against and takes a step away before speaking again. "From what I've seen so far, we're going to be good here, Rex. I don't foresee any problems at all with the others but if something does come up, we will handle it." He leaves me there to think about his reassurances.

I can't help but think about how hard we've all had to become since the bombs dropped. We went from a cushy life where the idea of taking a life was a shocking event that would cause a long-lasting ripple effect to ourselves and society, to it just being a sometimes needed event.

I'll never forget the first time after the bombs dropped that that lesson came hammering home.

Chapter Twelve ... Rex

Matty's smashing block towers in the corner with some of the toy blocks we brought with us from the store. The kid keeps building them up and knocking them down with great big belly laughs. I try and smile at his antics but the howling wind that smashes against the windows on the other side of the plywood covering them sends a frigid chill down my spine. You'd think I'd be used to it by now but even after four months of arctic weather it still gets to me.

Marsh and I are playing our thousandth round of cards while Sasha huddles under two blankets on the couch with a book. Lance, Ethan, and Belle are working on the garden they set up in the basement. I draw my next card and complete my winning hand but it's hard to get excited when you're numb. Not just numb from the constant cold but emotionally numb from being terrified for so long. Don't get me wrong, I feel safe with these people and I'm grateful they took Matty and me in but I still can't get over how everything has changed. My parents are dead and so is most of the world. Just about everything can kill you now, from the weather to the radiation or just other survivors. I've been waiting for four months for the next horror to happen and it's made me numb. I guess that's why I barely react when the back door comes smashing in, bringing a gust of arctic air and two huge monsters.

Sasha lets out a high pitched scream followed quickly by Matty's siren-like wail while Marsh and I just stare open mouthed with our cards still clutched in our hands. It takes a few seconds in the dim light for me to realize that they aren't monsters but two men bundled up in multiple layers of outerwear. The one in the lead pushes his hood off his head and quickly scans the room before focusing on Sasha and thrusting a gloved finger sharply at her with a harsh "shhh" sound. Her scream cuts off halfway through and she yanks the blankets up and over her head before he turns and faces Marsh and me.

He takes a step closer to us and into the flickering candle light we've been using to see our cards while the guy behind him wrestles with the damaged door to get it to close. His face is gaunt with his cheeks hollowed and his eyes sunken in, he looks half way to being a skeleton. This is the true face of what the bombs have left behind, starvation.

"Where's the food?" His voice rasps out menacingly. When no one answers him right away, he does the opposite of what I expect. I expect him to bellow and rage and threaten but instead, he lets out a deep sigh. "We know it's here. Every house in this area has been stripped of every crumb and you are the only ones living on this side of town. So, where's the food? You can give it to us or we can take it!"

I peel my eyes off of him to glance at Marsh to see if we should give this guy some of our supplies but he's looking past the intruders at something else. I swing my eyes back to the man and open my mouth to speak but whatever I was going to say comes out a gag as a bloody arrow tip explodes halfway out of his neck. I think the worst part of seeing my first man die is not the blood but the resignation and something that looks almost like relief in his eyes before he falls to the floor. It's almost like he's relieved he won't have to fight and struggle anymore.

When I finally pull my gaze from his empty eyes and look up, Belle is scooping Matty up and pulling Sasha off the couch before rushing them down into the basement. The second intruder is on his knees with Ethan gripping his shoulders from behind and Lance is in front of him with an arrow notched and ready to fly right at his face.

Marsh finally drops his cards to the table and stands but he moves towards the front of the house and looks out the viewing slot cut into the plywood over the window. I have no idea what I should be doing so I stay right where I am and watch the kneeling man's face. I'm amazed that there's no anger in the man's face. All I see is acceptance. Lance calmly asks the man questions about where he came from and if there are others in his group. When the man answers all of Lance's questions, I'm not even surprised by his response.

"You know we can't just let you go."

When the man merely nods, I finally realize that all of us are numb, not just me but everyone who's left.

I stay sitting there with my winning hand of cards clutched in my hand as Lance takes the man outside and Ethan works on fixing the damaged door. It isn't until Lance comes back and kneels in front of me and starts speaking that I finally move.

"Son, Rex, I need you to listen to me. What just happened was…sad. They were probably good men once but they had finally reached their limit and had become a danger to us and anyone else out there. The difference between us and them is a slim line but it's a line we will never cross. Life is hard now and it'll get much harder in the future but we will never attack and take food from other people so that we can survive. We have the smarts and will to take care of ourselves without resorting to that.

"Even if we had given them some of our supplies, it wouldn't have been enough. They would have come back for more eventually until it became a fight and we ended up having to kill them to keep us alive.

"I didn't enjoy doing that and I never will. Taking another's life is huge but this world has changed and we will do what it takes to keep our family alive. I want you and Marsh to really think about what happened here and what drove those men to try and take food from children. Listen to us and learn how to grow and hunt food so that you will never be forced to come close to that line. One day, and it will probably take years but one day, this world will be easier to live in again. "YOU need to decide what kind of man you'll be when that time comes. Will you be the man who killed others by stealing their food or will you be the man that learned how to survive honorably and killed only to protect yourself and your family?"

He leans back on his heels and waits for my response. I look down at the cards in my hand and for the first time since the bombs dropped, think that just maybe I was dealt a winning hand by ending up with these good people. I lay the cards down on the table and face him again before I nod in agreement and finally, I don't feel quite so numb anymore.

Chapter Thirteen ... Rex

The smell of baking bread has been wafting out of the kitchen all day and I'm ready to round up Matty and go sit down for whatever meal has been prepared for supper. I'm hauling the last bunk into place with Marsh when AIRIA's voice booms out to fill the cavern causing me to drop my end with a metallic clang to the concrete floor.

"Rex Larson, authorization increased to level green. Please proceed to alternate living quarters with Dr. Ethan Gains to attend to Skylar Ross and Benjamin Ross who are in medical distress."

It takes half a second for me to process this before I'm sprinting towards the offices. Medical distress? What does that mean? They're hurt, somehow they got hurt and need help. Ethan, I need Ethan! I change directions on the fly and almost skid out on my still damaged knee but ignore the flare of pain and keep going. I can hear pounding footsteps paralleling mine in a different area and when I clear the last set of bunks before the medical clinic I see Ethan disappearing through the doors. I fly towards the doors and make it through them before they slide closed.

Ethan has a bag in hand and is throwing supplies into it while talking to AIRIA.

"AIRIA, what happened to Skylar and Benjamin? Is it trauma or illness? What are their symptoms?"

"Dr. Ethan Gains, it appears to be an illness of some kind. Symptoms are dangerously elevated temperatures and respiratory congestion. Without fluid samples, I am unable to reach a further diagnosis."

I stand waiting for him - but all I want to do is run. Run to Sky's place and make sure she and Ben are okay. I know he needs to take supplies with us but inside my head, I'm screaming "LET'S GO!" He finally looks up from a drawer that he's pulling I.V. bags from and notices me waiting for him.

"Oh, Rex, good, you're here! Take this bag so I can start filling another one."

I snatch the bag from him but grab his arm as he starts to move away.

"Ethan, we have to go! We can come back for more if you need it. Or we can bring them both here!"

Ethan stares at me for a second before he starts shaking his head. "No, we aren't going to do that. Skylar does not want to be over here and she really doesn't want her brother here. We are not going to go against her wishes on that if I can help it. Bring what you have in that bag and I'll come back for more if I need to."

I turn without a word and wait impatiently as the doors slide open before sprinting towards the offices. I see faces staring at me as I run past including a worried looking Belle and Matty, but I can't stop. Skylar and Ben need help and it's my turn to do the saving. Ethan and I run down the corridor to the double metal doors. There always seems to be doors between me and Sky but this time she's given me the key so my palm slaps the pad and the doors slide soundlessly open. Our feet echo even louder in the tunnel and it feels like I'm running in place. I'm so scared of what we'll find on the other end.

The tunnel doors open between the animal area and the gardens and I have to stop and take a few steps back to get Ethan moving again because he's standing there staring at the small farm. He shakes away his amazement and starts following me again. Over the small bridge and past Ben's sandbox, then palming the door to their living quarters. I scan the living room and kitchen but there's no one there so I take a right and see a foot on the ground just inside Ben's bedroom.

My heart just stops with my feet when I get close enough to see her laying on the floor. How could this happen so fast? I just saw her less than twenty-four hours ago! Ethan shoves me out of the way and hits the carpet on his knees beside her. He's checking for a pulse on her neck and yelling at me but all I can see is Sky laying there on the floor lifeless and it's frozen me solid.

Ethan breaks me from my trance by wrenching the bag of medical supplies from my shoulder and I finally hear what he's saying.

"Rex, she's breathing! Help me get her off the floor!"

I shake off my shock and help him get Sky onto the bed beside Ben. I can feel the heat radiating off of them both and it scares me to death how limp and lifeless Sky is when we lift her. I stand there feeling useless while Ethan pulls out a stethoscope and listens to both of their chests. My whole body is vibrating with the need to DO something, anything but this is beyond my abilities to fix so I have to just trust Ethan to make them better. He finally stands up and turns to me.

"Rex, I'm going to start I.V.'s for both of them and get some antibiotics running. I think it's pneumonia but can't know for sure unless I can do some x-ray's back at the clinic. I'm almost positive though because there was a little girl in the hotel group who I think has it also. Her x-rays showed cloudy lungs so I set her up on an I.V. with antibiotics earlier this morning. Skylar probably picked it up from her and passed it on to Ben. They've been so isolated all these years that any bug is going to knock them right off their feet and move quicker than in people who have a better developed immune system. I need you to go back to the clinic and get a stretcher so we can move them."

I just stare down at the two of them without moving. I did this to them. I remember how fierce Skylar was the first time she brought me and Matty into the airlock. How she was afraid we would infect Ben with something from the outside because he's never been exposed to any real germs before. I remember her carrying a little girl on our mad run to get inside when the rain started and how she told AIRIA to override the decontamination process to get us all in faster.

I did this to them. For the second time, I brought danger into her home and put the only thing that matters to her at risk. How will she ever begin to forgive me? I don't think she will. The only thing I can do is pray that Ethan can get them better so I ask the computer.

"AIRIA, is there a stretcher here on this side of the tunnel?"

"Rex Larson, a medical stretcher can be found in storage container A1."

I back away from the bed, not wanting to take my eyes off the girl I know I've lost for good. Ethan squeezes my arm and I make myself stop thinking. There will be time later, once they're better, to face my guilt. Then I'm running out the door again.

Ethan doesn't want to leave either of them alone so we put them both on the stretcher with their heads at either end. I'm thankful that it's a full ambulance style stretcher with folding legs and wheels so we can move them faster and safer than trying to carry them both. Ben opens his eyes briefly when we lift him onto the stretcher, but I don't think he's really with us. Skylar stays limp and doesn't even moan. I can't help but wonder if all the pain and stress she's endured since I came into her life has left her weakened. She's such a fighter so it seems absurd that something as small as a germ can bring her down.

I'm so lost in thought that I don't even realize that we've made it through the tunnel and to the metal doors until Ethan has to ask me to palm it open. Lance is waiting on the other side when the door opens.

"Guys, how bad is it? Belle has set up two beds in the clinic for them to be moved to."

Ethan shakes his head and waves him out of the way to get the stretcher moving again before responding.

"They need chest x-rays. I'm pretty sure it's pneumonia but the x-ray will tell me for sure. If that's what it is, we'll be taking them back to their area and I'll stay and monitor them there."

Lance is following along beside us as we pass even more people standing and watching us. I see Sasha in the group and pray she doesn't have a happy or satisfied expression on her face or I might not be able to control my reaction. Thankfully she's just frowning as we go by so I push her from my head and focus on what comes next.

"Why can't they just stay here in the clinic? Are they contagious?" Lance asks as we pause to let the clinic's doors slide open.

Ethan doesn't bother to answer but moves over to a cupboard and grabs a few face masks and starts handing them out. He lines the stretcher up against one of the beds and gently moves Ben over to it and adjusts his I.V. before turning and pushing Skylar towards the x-ray room. Just as he goes through with her he calls over his shoulder to us.

"Rex, wash your hands with soap and the rest of you get out!"

I do as he says but Lance and Belle just wait for him to come back out. When I turn around after drying my hands I see the woman and little girl who Skylar, Marsh and I helped from outside. Her face is sad when she meets my gaze over her own paper mask. She must realize it was her daughter that made Skylar and Ben sick. I don't know what to say to her so I just nod and turn to the others.

"Why can't they stay here, Rex? That other little girl is sick too. It makes sense for Ethan to have all the patients in one place." Lance asks.

I want nothing more than to have Sky and Ben here close to me so I can stay and watch over them but I know that I can't put my feelings ahead of what Sky wants. I'm the reason they're sick so I'll honor her wishes no matter what. I explain to Lance and Belle. Belle's nodding in understanding but Lance doesn't agree.

"I get that she doesn't want to be a part of our group but they're sick. They need to be here in the clinic!" Lance counters.

Before I have a chance to reply, Ethan is wheeling Skylar back into the room. He must have caught some of what we were talking about because he immediately shuts Lance down.

"No, I'll be taking them back to their living area as soon as I get the results back from some tests." He maneuvers her stretcher next to Ben's and heads over to the cabinets to start preparing medicine.

Lance is scowling and takes a step towards Ethan's turned back.

"Ethan, be reasonable!"

Ethan drops what he's working on and turns to face us. He sighs and tugs down his paper mask so it hangs around his neck before replying.

"Yes, it would be more convenient to have them both over here but it also would have been more convenient and safer for Skylar to have left us outside. This little girl has had to endure a lot of pain and upset since we came into her life. She's been carrying the load of her brother's safety and well-being entirely on her shoulders. All she wanted in return for all that she did for us is to be left alone to continue that. I don't agree with her because I think it's time she let others help her share that load but I will honor her wishes until she comes to that decision." He glances over at Sky and Ben and rubs at his tired face. "From what I've seen and heard about her so far, Skylar is a very special person. She needs help but she needs to come to that on her own. Forcing it on her might break her. I honestly think she's close to a breakdown. The first time I met her in the cavern, she was half way to a full blown panic attack. You can only live under so much stress for so long before something has to give, especially at her age. I won't be the one to break her just so I'm not inconvenienced."

Belle's nodding her head in agreement but Lance is frowning.

"Yeah, we owe her for taking us in. I guess this is a good way of building up trust with her and I think we'll need to have that trust. I think things are going to start changing outside soon. All the forecasts I had read in the army about the aftermath of a full out nuclear war, stated that the timeframe of the atmosphere clearing would be between seven to ten years. I think the rain is the start of it. Skylar might have knowledge or access to things that will help us all start reclaiming a real life outside once it's safe. We're going to have to start making plans for a future outside. I very much want that girl to be a part of those plans."

Lance looks at all of us in turn with love and sadness on his face.

"The past seven years has been a struggle for all of us but we had each other to count on and make a life with. Skylar had the opposite. She had the luxuries of everyday needs but she's had to do it all alone while growing up and learning to parent her brother at the same time." He looks to me, "Her father gave you, Matty, Belle, and Sasha a huge advantage the day the bombs dropped and it probably saved all your lives. We owe it to him to take care of his children now in any way we can."

Ethan nods his head and turns away to work on the medicine that will hopefully make Sky and Ben healthy again. Lance and Belle leave the clinic to go back to the work they had been doing earlier and I pull up a chair next to Sky's stretcher and just wait for her to wake up.

...

"Is Sky going to die, Rex?"

I lift my tired head from the side of Sky's bed where I've been for the last three days and turn to look at her little brother on the stretcher bed we had brought into her room so they could be together. He's very pale and dark circles stand out under his scared and sad eyes but thankfully, the red flush from fever has left his cheeks.

"No buddy, she's not! She's just sleeping now. Ethan said her last chest x-ray showed improvement."

Ben scrunches his face up in worry. "Then how come she's not waking up? I woke up yesterday."

I turn back to look at Sky's peacefully sleeping face. I don't really know what to tell him. She should have woken up by now. The medicine Ethan started them on had worked to bring their fevers down and started to clear their lungs after the first twenty-four hours. Ben had woken up not long after that but Sky's closed eyes hadn't even so much as fluttered so I tell him the only thing I can think of.

"I think she's just really tired and needs her rest to get better. She'll be ok, little man."

Ben's voice hitches with tears, "I think it's my fault. I was really mean to her. I said lots of mean things to her before she let all you guys in. Maybe she's mad at me and that's why she won't wake up."

His voice is so sad and his words echo the guilt I have in my own head and heart.

"No Ben, that's not it at all. It's my fault you guys got sick. It was some of the people who came inside with me that were sick and gave it to Sky." I lower my head back to the side of the bed and close my eyes before whispering. "All I've done since meeting you guys is bring danger into your home. I'm so sorry Ben."

I must have fallen asleep for a while because the next thing I know is Ethan's shaking my shoulder and motioning me out of the room. I take a last look at Sky but she's still out and Ben's sleeping too, so I follow Ethan out into the living room. Ethan looks just as tired as I feel but I hope he got some sleep on the couch. We've both been taking shifts staying with Sky and Ben and after three days it's starting to wear us down.

"I'd like to take Ben over to the clinic for another chest x-ray and blood draw to check his numbers. He seems to be improving but I'm worried about his kidneys being damaged. I'll do Skylar's after his. You need to spend a little time with your own brother while we're over there. He's probably getting pretty worried about you."

I try and rub away the exhaustion from my face as I think about Matty for the first time in hours. Ethan's right. Even with the others to watch over him, I should check on him but I hate the idea of leaving Sky over here alone.

"What about Sky? Do you really think she's ok to be left alone? I just don't understand why she hasn't woken up yet!"

Ethan walks over and gently closes the bedroom door before answering me.

"There is no medical reason for Skylar to have not woken up yet. Ben's pneumonia was worse than hers was and he woke up in under a day after I started their IV antibiotics."

"I think, well - I don't think she wants to wake up yet." At my confused look, he sighs.

"Honestly, I think Skylar is tired, mentally. She's had so much heaped on her shoulders for so long that I think she's taking a break, for want of a better term. She needs to want to wake up, so once we finish running the tests and get back here, we should have Ben start talking to her. There are plenty of reports in the medical community of patients waking up and reporting that they heard their loved ones speaking to them while they were in a coma or unconscious. We'll see if Ben can reach her. As for her staying over here alone, I don't think she's in any danger now but I will ask AIRIA to keep monitoring her and alert us if her vital signs start to go bad. I wish you could stay here but only you are authorized to open the doors for us."

I glance back at the closed bedroom door before reluctantly agreeing. I hate the idea of leaving her for even a few minutes.

"I guess there's no choice but to leave her alone for a bit. I need to milk the cow and collect the eggs so I'll grab Matty and bring him over for that. The kid should get a kick out of it."

Ethan's expression turns thoughtful before asking,

"How much milk and eggs are you getting from that every day? What have you been doing with it all?"

"Well, there's quite a lot in the walk in fridge in their storage area that's just sitting there. I don't know how long the milk will last before it goes bad. There's probably two dozen eggs by now in the basket on top of the dozens already in the storage room. Skylar said something about canning and dehydrating them when she gave me a tour when we first got here but I can't remember exactly what that was all about. Why? What are you thinking?"

Ethan leans against the back of the couch and folds his arms. "If Skylar and Ben aren't using the fresh dairy products and they'll just spoil anyways, do you think she would be upset if we took them to the barracks to use? There are some kids over there that would really benefit from fresh milk. I worry about the lack of calcium that you kids have missed growing up. Would you give me a quick tour of the storage and fridge over here? I don't want to take her supplies but if it's just going to spoil anyways then she shouldn't mind."

I nod. "When Sky first showed me around, I asked her about all the extra fresh food she was producing that she and Ben couldn't use up. That's when she explained about the canning and dehydrating she does. She said that even though there are huge amounts of supplies in here that at some point they would be living outside and helping to rebuild. She's been preserving all this stuff to help others in the future. I think she would hate for the milk and eggs to spoil instead of giving it to us so I think it's ok to take some of it."

Ethan pushes away from the couch with a nod. "Ok, let's take a quick look in that fridge and load up a cart with some milk and eggs to take over to the barracks. You can push it to the tunnel while I go get Ben into the wheelchair for the trip over to the clinic."

I show Ethan the contents of the storage room and walk-in fridge and smile at his look of wonder. I figure it's the same expression that was on my face the day Sky had first shown me everything. I have to laugh when his mouth drops open in shock when he sees the area in storage that has chocolate. After seven years of living off of the most basic of food supplies and lots and lots of sprouts, seeing such luxuries that we used to take for granted was kind of awe inspiring.

It doesn't take long for us to fill a push cart with jugs of milk with thick cream settled on top. We only take the oldest jugs and leave the fresher ones in the fridge. We both look longingly at the baskets of fresh produce but neither one of us is willing to take what Sky and Ben had produced with hard work without permission. She's already done so much for us at a huge cost to her and Ben that we won't take advantage of anything else.

When Ethan joins me at the tunnel entrance with Ben in a wheelchair, I ask him about the milk but he just shrugs his shoulders and says "Sure", so we head through the tunnel to the barracks. I can't help but look over my shoulder back toward where we left Sky all alone.

Chapter Fourteen ... Skylar

"How do I look?"

I spin around on my silver ballet flat slipper, making my gorgeous silver and gold prom dress flare out in glimmering waves. My long blond hair is perfectly curled with half of it swept up on top of my head with jeweled combs. I've never felt so beautiful in all my life.

"Oh, Sky! Oh my baby, all grown up! You look just like a princess!"

I laugh at the sentimental tears filling Mom's eyes and feel my own eyes growing damp. I quickly blink them away though. She's let me use mascara for the first time and there's no way I'm ruining it with tears.

"There's NO WAY you're leaving this house looking that gorgeous! Especially with a BOY!" bellows Dad in fake outrage, making me giggle. He shakes his head in wonder and makes a twirling motion with his finger so I spin around again. I can feel the glow of happiness on my face as the dress settles back down over my knees.

I'm so excited I can barely contain myself and I just want to bounce up and down and clap my hands in glee. This is my very first dance that I'm going to and I can't wait for my date to get here and see me in my dress.

Ben does the bouncing and clapping for me as he dances around me chanting, "Princess Sky, Princess Sky!"

Dad clears his throat and lifts the camera up to his face to take more pictures but not before I see he has tears in his eyes as well.

"Skylar Ross, perimeter breach detected."

A frown crosses Dad's face and we all freeze for an instant but then the doorbell rings through the house making me jump in excitement.

"He's here!"

I take a few quick steps towards the door before spinning around and pointing a teasingly stern finger at Dad.

"BE NICE!" I say before I dash off to open the door. Another giggle erupts from my mouth when I hear him mutter, "No promises."

I get to the door and pause to straighten my dress and pat at my hair. I wonder if he'll be able to hear the pounding of my excited heart. I can't help but smile even wider as I open the door and see him standing there in his tux with flowers in his hands. My belly flutters at the admiring look in his green eyes and his dimples deepen when his own smile widens. The limo I can see waiting at the curb behind him just sweetens the whole night and we haven't even made it to the dance yet.

We just stand there smiling at each other like a couple of loons until I feel my dad's hands land on my shoulders.

"Skylar, do you want to let Rex in now or are you guys just going to stand there all night?"

Rex turns bright red and another giggle slips out of me before I step back and move to the side. Rex juggles the flowers to get a free hand and thrusts it towards my dad who's standing there with his arms crossed and a scowl on his face.

"Mr. Ross, thank you for letting me take your daughter to the prom tonight. I promise to take good care of her!"

We both wait anxiously until dad finally cracks a smile and shakes Rex's hand.

"You better take care of her and no funny business Mister!" He practically growls but his grin takes the sting out of his words. He's known Rex since he was ten and has always had a soft spot for him.

"Daniel, stop terrorizing the boy and let him in! I want to get some pictures of the kids together before they leave."

Dad tugs Rex into the house and mock growls over his shoulder at Mom, "It's a father's duty to terrorize his daughter's suitors, Vanessa. Don't you remember your father putting me through the wringer when we started dating?"

Mom just laughs and pulls Rex and me into position before snapping a kazillion pictures. Once Rex has pinned my corsage to my dress with shaking hands, it's time to go. He holds out his arm with his elbow bent for me and we head to the door. We only make it halfway there when from the ceiling a computer voice blares out.

"Skylar Ross, attempted breach of barracks exterior door detected. Integrity maintained."

My parents' faces change in an instant. They were happy and proud but now Mom starts weeping and Dad's face is full of anger. He lunges towards us and yanks me away from Rex.

"Skylar, I told you not to trust anyone! What are you doing? Are you trying to get Ben killed? How could you be so careless?"

I stare at him in shock. What? What does he mean? I look to Mom for help but she's on the floor in a puddle of blood. I spin frantically in a circle trying to understand and now I see Dad lying on the carpet naked with a bullet hole in his back. My mouth opens and a sound I've never heard before comes rushing out. It's the sound of a wounded animal. My eyes see Ben on the ground also. He's not moving and I don't know if he's alive. Finally, my horrified eyes find Rex and he's standing there in the middle of my decimated family shaking his head saying he's sorry over and over again.

My knees hit the carpet and I tear at the beautiful gown that just moments ago I was so proud to wear. There is no beauty in this world. There's only death. My parents are dead but I need to get to Ben so I throw myself towards him only to come face first with the carpet.

I push myself up on weak shaking arms and look through blurry eyes at the empty bedroom I'm in. There's no one here. I'm not in the house I grew up in but in my bedroom in the cave. My parents are long gone and Rex isn't here with me but neither is Benny. I use the side of the bed to claw myself to my feet on legs that barely hold me up. I have to find Ben! The dream is still with me, giving me the adrenaline I need to stagger to the door. I clutch at the frame to stay upright and use the wall as support to make my way to Benny's room but land on my knees again when I find it empty. I'm having a hard time getting my breath so when I try and speak nothing comes out but a wheeze.

My throat and mouth are so dry I can barely swallow so I crawl to the kitchen and use the counter to pull myself up where I hang over the sink and nudge the faucet open. The first sip from my shaking, cupped hand is heaven even as the majority of the water slides down my face and soaks into my shirt. I keep taking tiny sips from my cupped hand until my stomach starts to hurt so I just lay my cheek against the cool counter and try and get my breathing under control. My chest hurts with every breath but slowly my heart starts to settle down and the pressure on my lungs becomes bearable. I open my eyes and try to stand upright but the world tilts dizzyingly so I put my head back down again.

I have never felt so wretched in my whole life but I need to get it under control and find Ben. The last memory I have that wasn't a dream was of Ben passed out on the floor. Anything that happened after that is a blank. I don't know how I ended up in my room or where Ben is and I have to fight hard to keep the panic I'm feeling from overwhelming my body. Based on how weak and shaky I feel, I've been sick and I don't know how long I was out. I need answers. My voice is nothing more than a hoarse croak but it's enough.

"AIRIA, where is Ben?"

"Skylar Ross, Benjamin Ross is located in the barracks."

Frack! What's he doing over there? I told him how I felt about us mixing with the other people and he went and…wait, "AIRIA, Ben's not authorized to open those doors! Who opened the doors for him?"

"Skylar Ross, Rex Larson, authorization level green, opened the doors."

What the frack is going on? How long have I been out of it? My head's spinning now physically and mentally from confusion. I try again.

"AIRIA, how did Rex get a green authorization and how long was I out of it?"

"Skylar Ross, you approved Rex Larson's authorization level and you have been unconscious for three days and six hours."

Holy crap, none of this makes sense so I'll figure it out later. Right now I need to get Ben back. I need to see him with my own eyes to make sure he's safe. I push slowly upright this time and manage to keep my balance so I carefully work my way down the counter and get across the gap to the bathroom where I take care of some much-needed business. After washing my face and teeth and sipping more water, I start to feel somewhat better. I know I'm not going to make it very far in my condition but I'm willing to take that chance to get Ben back where he belongs. I can push through this and collapse after that. I catch a whiff of three days' worth of the same clothes and decide to remedy that before going to the barracks.

Using the kitchen counter again to steady myself, I stop and pull a stale bun from a container on the counter as well as a juice box from the cupboard. I figure even a few bites will help bolster my strength and the sugar in the juice will help as well. I nibble away at the bun as I make my way back to my room and change into non-stinky clothes before strapping on my holster and gun from the closet. When Ben's safety is a concern, I will no longer take any chances. I don't know what's going on in the barracks but it's time I stopped being the sad, sucky girl I've been for the last week or so and got back to being the strong, fierce protector of Ben. It's time I took control and this time I plan on keeping it!

By the time I'm at the door to the tunnel, I've finished my bun and juice and feel steadier on my feet. I'm definitely still very sick but I feel like I'm strong enough for right now to do whatever I need to, to get Ben back. I take a minute to rest and steady my breathing again when I get to the barracks entrance. I don't remember the tunnel being so long and I need a minute before I go through.

Once I'm rested and feel stronger again, I palm open the door and step through into the office area. I head down the hall to the barracks without another thought. Ben's in there somewhere and I'm going to do whatever it takes to bring him home.

My eyes widen in shock when I see how different the barracks are from the last time I was in here. I grip the door frame and scan the huge area for any sign of my brother. All the bunks have been moved into groups leaving huge open areas that have been filled with tables. To my eyes, so long unaccustomed to seeing other people, it seems like there are hundreds of them moving around the different areas. I feel my chest tighten up even more than it already is with claustrophobia. I need to go out there in those crowds to find Ben. I shove the fear aside and push off from the frame and head straight to the middle area that used to be filled with bunks. It has the most people there and someone is going to tell me where to find my brother.

I grit my teeth against the feeling that the walls and ceiling are getting closer as I step closer and closer to the crowd of people. I try and swallow the dryness in my throat away so I can yell my questions without getting too close but all the water I drank seems to have disappeared from my body. I'm going to have to get closer.

I move a little further until I'm only about ten feet from one of the new tables that have people I don't recognise sitting at it but before I have a chance to call out, my arm is grabbed and I'm being swung around.

"What do you think ***you're*** doing here? What happened to, "this is your side and that's my side"? I guess Queen Skylar doesn't have to follow her own rules, huh?"

She's spitting out the words as she spins me around and just finishing her condescending sentence when I come face to face with her. My gun's in my hand the minute she grabbed my arm and the follow through brings the barrel upright between her eyes. Eyes that go from hurtful and nasty to wide and terrified. For as much as my legs feel like they are shaky noodles, my hand is rock steady. This is a target I can focus on. This is pain and suffering and fear. This took away any chance I had for a happier future. The hoarseness of my dry throat makes my words come out even more threatening than I had planned.

"Where is my brother?"

Her hand comes up halfway like she's going to plead with me to stop and her head gives a tiny shake like she's afraid to do more. I take a half step closer to her so the barrel of my gun is only an inch away from her forehead and raise my eyebrow. I won't ask again.

Somewhere deep inside of me I'm horrified at what I'm doing and I fear that after killing Ted, the second one won't be as hard. As I wait for an answer my mind goes through a good angel, bad angel routine. Does this girl really deserve to die for what she's done? Do I take a chance that she'll do something even worse in the future? Am I really a cold blooded killer now? Am I willing to do whatever it takes to protect myself and Ben?

Before any of these questions can be answered, I see movement rushing towards me and a loud voice starts to call out.

"Whoa, ladies, cool your coconuts! Mellow your melons! ***Hakuna*** your ***tatas***!"

I haven't taken my eyes off of Sasha, so I see the changes of expression on her face that must exactly match my own, amazed disbelief that morphs into outrage. We both turn our heads towards him at the exact same time. There's Marsh with his hands up and a huge fake grin that shows all of his teeth. Did he just say…?

I turn my head back to Sasha and she's looking me in the eye but no longer terrified by the gun pointed at her head. Instead, she gets a small smirk on her face and says,

"Can you shoot him instead? Maybe just a little bit? Like in the leg?"

I feel my own lips tug up towards a grin in sisterly solidarity and it's enough to bring me out of the dangerous haze I was in. I let the gun fall to my side and holster it. In seconds it feels like it weighs a hundred pounds. I give Sasha a weary nod and turn to look for Ben again. He's the reason I'm here, not my quarrel with Sasha. What I see brings the panic and claustrophobia roaring back. Faces surround me. They're all looking at me with frowns of disapproval or angry expressions. I try and spin away but they are all around me and I feel the giant cavern start pressing down on me. I try and find a break in the crowd so I can run but it's a wall of people and they're ALL STARING AT ME! My breathing turns to gasps as my chest tightens and I fight for every breath.

There, there's movement and the crowd starts to part so I lunge towards it only to come to a stop because there's Ben. He's in a wheelchair and his expression is one I've never seen before. It's like he doesn't even know me. That doctor is standing behind him holding the handles of his chair. He's talking to me but all I can see is the look on Ben's face and I can't bear it so I look away and then there's Rex. Rex, who wants to be with me and wants to talk to me and work things out, except this Rex looks disgusted with me. I can barely breathe now and all those faces are starting to blur and the ceiling is pressing down against my head and all I can do is RUN!

I push through the blurry angry faces and stagger free but the ceiling is still coming down so I hunch my shoulders and move my broken body as fast as I can back towards the offices and then the tunnel. I think I hear someone calling my name but it's hard to hear over the roaring sound of the ceiling coming down so I just stagger on. I bounce from wall to wall until I can't go any further and my legs give out and I fall down to the cold concrete floor of the tunnel. I just lay there and wait to suffocate. My lungs aren't working anymore but that doesn't matter because the ceiling is all the way down and about to crush me. It's over, so I just let go and hope I'll be with Mom and Dad soon.

Chapter Fifteen ... Rex

Ethan takes Ben over to the clinic while I push the cart full of milk jugs to the kitchen. By the way the people working in the kitchen reacted, you would think I was delivering molten gold instead of fresh milk. I swear, one of the women even has tears in her eyes. I tell them that Ethan recommended that the milk be given out to all children and everyone happily agrees.

I leave the kitchen in search of my brother with a satisfied feeling but wishing Skylar was here to see just how happy her unknown contributions have made people. As I walk through the barracks I can't help but feel proud of the way these people have all come together since we arrived to organize and create a functioning home. The sign-up sheets Lance had created and printed from the office computers are full of people who want to work. The garden growing area is already full of soil and seeds from the bags taken from the storage containers. The cooking and cleaning lists have plenty of volunteers signed up so no one person is stuck with all the grunt work. So far everyone is getting along and happy to have such a safe place to stay but I wonder if it will stay that way. At the hotel, all these people were kept under Ted and his men's heavy thumb so no one dared to cause any trouble. I worry that once the shine of safety and comfort wears off there might be issues.

As I scan the different groups for Matty, I put it out of my mind for now. I have enough to worry about with Sky being so sick.

A small body hurtles into me from the side causing me to stagger. Looks like the kid's found me instead. I snatch him up and throw him over my shoulder and spin around causing him to laugh like a loon before depositing him back on his feet.

"REX! Are you back for good? Is Skylar and Ben all better? Can I see Ben?"

"Whoa there pal! Ben's doing a lot better and he's over in the clinic with Ethan getting another x-ray so yes, we can go visit with him for a few minutes before he heads back to his place. Skylar, well, she's still pretty sick so I'm going back over to stay with her for a while more." I tell him and give his messy hair a rub.

He frowns at the news that I'm going back so I tell him my plan. "I really need your help but I'm not sure if you're old enough to help me."

"Yes, I am! I'm totally old enough for…uhh what is it?"

I laugh at this instant declaration even when he doesn't know what I'm asking. "Well, Sky and Ben's animals need to be looked after. The cow needs to be milked and its stall needs to be cleaned out. The chickens need to be fed and the eggs collected as well. Do you think you're big enough to handle that with me?"

Matty places his hands on his hips and scowls at me. "Of course I am! Ben showed me how to do it already when they first gave us the tour over there. It's easy! I don't even need you to do it with me. I can do it all by myself!"

I throw my arm around his neck in a loose headlock and pull him along with me towards the clinic.

"Yeah, yeah, I'm sure you could manage a whole farm by yourself but I think I'll stick around to help out this time. Come on Farmer Joe, let's go see if Ethan's ready to head back over yet."

Ben easily slips out of the headlock and starts strutting beside me while pretending to have his thumbs stuck under imaginary suspenders. He has me chuckling with his sad attempt at a farmer's accent. "HYuck, hyuk, hyuk. I'm Farmer Joe and I'm gonna milk me some cows."

We've just reached the clinic's doors when I hear raised voices coming from the center of the barracks. I turn to look back and my mouth drops. That's Sky over there and she's pointing a gun at someone's head! The crowd shifts and I get a look at who it is. I curse under my breath, of course, it's Sasha. I'm thrilled to see Sky awake and on her feet but the gun in her hand has me panicking. I can just image what she felt when she woke up and found Ben missing. I'm about to sprint over to them when the doors behind me open up and Ethan pushes Ben through in his wheelchair. I yell at him over my shoulder, even as I start running.

"Sky's over there and she's got a gun! Bring Ben so she knows he's ok!"

I figure I'll beat them to Sky and get her calmed down but it seems like every person in the barracks has moved into my way so by the time I push a path through the crowd Ethan and Ben are right on my heels. The crowd finally parts all the way and I get a good up close look at Sky. She's lowering her gun and puts it back into her holster but she looks awful. I can tell something is seriously wrong right away. Her chest is hitching like she's just run a marathon and her face is paper white with black and blue circles under her eyes. But it's what's in her eyes that worry me the most. They're full of terror and confusion. She spins around in a circle like a trapped animal trying to find a way to escape until her eyes find Ben.

Ethan tries to calm her down.

"Skylar, it's ok! I was just taking Ben for an x-ray and then bringing him right back. You've both been very sick."

I can tell she's not hearing him at all. Her eyes dart away from Ben and meet mine. What I see in them breaks my heart. She's lost in confusion and panic and I don't think she even really sees me in front of her. There's small agonizing gasps coming from her that scare me. She's way too sick to be trying to deal with any of this. I go to reach out to her but she spins away and charges through the crowd with her shoulders hunched over like she thinks someone's going to hit her at any moment.

"SKY, Skylar!" I shout after her but she keeps going back towards the offices. I turn to Ethan and see that Ben is sobbing.

"We have to go after her. She's not thinking straight! Bring Ben, she's going to need to see that he's ok."

I don't wait for an answer, just spin and chase after her. I can't believe she's even still on her feet let alone running, after being unconscious for three days but she disappears into the office hallway ahead of me. I hit the hallway at top speed and immediately crash into Lance sending us both to the floor. I try and scramble away from him but he grabs me by the arms and holds me still.

"What the hell is going on? Was that Skylar I just saw running past? She doesn't look very good!"

"Let go! I've got to get to her, Lance. She doesn't know what she's doing right now. She needs help!"

I finally shake off his hands, stumble to my feet and lunge to the tunnel doors. As soon as they slide open I see her. She's not even half way back to her side and she's laying on the concrete floor. No, no, no, she has to be ok! I reach her in seconds and drop down beside her. My hands reach out to touch her but they freeze half way. Her eyes are open but they're fixed on somewhere that's not here. She's on her side in the fetal position with her arms crossed in front of her chest. Her whole body jerks with every hitch of her chest as she tries to force air into her lungs. I know it's not working because her lips have a blue tinge to them.

I've seen a lot of damaged people since the bombs dropped but never like this. I don't know how to fix this but I hope Ethan can. I reach over and slide my arms underneath her and gently cradle her against my chest before pushing to my feet. I'm afraid of jostling her if I run, even though both my heart and head are screaming for me to move fast. So I walk quickly instead back towards the barracks. I'm not letting go of her even with one hand so when I get a few feet from the door I yell at the computer.

"AIRIA, open the tunnel door."

The doors start sliding open even as the reply comes.

"Rex Larson, Skylar Ross's vital signs are deteriorating quickly. Medical treatment is needed."

I don't bother responding because the doors open revealing Ethan and Ben in his wheelchair on the other side.

"Rex, I'm not authorized to open…" He takes one look at Skylar and stops what he was going to say. Instead, he turns Ben's chair around and pushes it towards Lance who is standing there with them.

"Take Ben into our suite and keep him there. He doesn't need to see his sister like this!"

Without even looking at Lance for his reply, he's turned back to me and reaching for Sky's neck to check her pulse. His face tells me all I need to know and we both start moving as fast as I can with Skylar in my arms. I ignore Ben's screaming for his sister as Ethan's yelling ahead of us for people to get out of the way. I don't even see them because my eyes are locked on the doors of the clinic and hopefully what's on the other side can save this sad broken girl.

"On the bed, on the bed, Rex!" Ethan's yelling the minute the clinic doors open. He's a whirlwind of activity as he turns a valve to an oxygen mask and quickly slides it on to Sky's face. He's hooking up machines to her that I don't understand and I just stand there waiting for something good to magically happen. Once the beeps fill the room Ethan stares at a machine and chants under his breath, "Come on, come on Skylar, breathe."

He shoots a look my way and his frown deepens. "You should leave, Rex. If her oxygen levels don't come up, I might have to intubate her. That's not something you want to see."

I just give my head a hard shake. "I'm not going anywhere! I don't understand what happened. She seemed ok a few minutes ago!"

Ethan shakes his head. "No, she wasn't. I imagine that display out there was her running on pure adrenalin. Her lungs are already bad enough, with pneumonia, so she was pushing past her limits with that - but I'm almost certain based on her reactions that she was having a severe panic attack and hyperventilated on top of it. Her body just shut itself down to try and survive. I think she must have woken up confused and when she couldn't find Ben it sent her into a spin. This is probably the break that I thought was coming." He turns back to the monitors and his shoulders slump. "I'm sorry Rex. We shouldn't have left her."

I've got nothing to say to his apology because I feel the same. I should never have left her alone. I've got so much guilt on my shoulders for what Sky's been through. As much as she's done for me and mine is how much damage I've done to her. I just want her to get better so I can ask for her forgiveness.

All I can do is sit and watch as Ethan re-attaches an IV to her pale lifeless arm and starts injecting it with medicine. I'm in a haze of despair as people come and go and Ethan tries to tell me everything he's doing but none of it means anything to me until I see a slight flutter of her eyelids. I hold my breath until they slowly open to reveal her confused sleepy blue eyes. My breath whooshes out of me and a slight grin tugs at my lips but before it forms she starts struggling and tries to pull the oxygen mask from her face.

Ethan grabs her arm and pulls it away causing her to start thrashing in panic. I jump to my feet from the chair beside her bed and lean over her so all she can see is my face and I talk slow and loud.

"Skylar, calm down! Everything is ok. You are ok. Ben is ok. You need to stay still and listen to me!"

Her body stops struggling but her eyes are full of fear when they meet mine. I brush her cheek with the back of my hand and try and explain what has happened.

"You and Ben have pneumonia but Ethan has been treating you both with medicine. We knew you didn't want Ben to be over here so Ethan and I have been staying with both of you over at your place for the last three days. Ben responded to the medicine faster and started to get better first. There is an x-ray machine over here in the clinic so we brought him over for a chest scan to look at his lungs and then we were bringing him right back. You must have woken up right after we left and panicked. I'm sorry I left you alone but Ethan doesn't have the authorization to open the tunnel door so I had to go with him to let him and Ben through."

Her forehead furrows in a frown but her slight nod lets me know she's understanding me so far. Ethan had let her arm go when she calmed down so she lifts it to the mask on her face again. I gently capture her hand before she can pull it off and keep explaining.

"You have to leave that on right now. Your lungs are having a hard time so you need the oxygen to get better. Ethan thinks you might have had a panic attack and hyperventilated so you really need the oxygen."

Her voice is muffled under the mask but I can still make out her words. "The ceiling was coming down. It was going to crush me."

I shoot a quick glance at Ethan and he gives a grim nod of understanding before moving forward into Skylar's field of vision. Her eyes track to him as he starts talking.

"Hi Skylar, we met briefly on the day you let us in. I'm Ethan and I'm a doctor. Ben is doing great. He responded nicely to the medicine I gave him and is quickly recovering. I don't want you to worry about him right now. I promise you that we will keep him safe and get him healthy as quick as we can. Right now we need to worry about you. Pneumonia hit you very hard and I'm worried about the damage you might have done to your lungs. As soon as you've rested a bit, I'd like to get a chest scan and draw some blood. I know this is hard for you but you need to let me take care of you." Ethan's face softens and he gently takes her hand free hand in his. "Sweetie, I know it's been your job to take care of Ben but you really need to let us help you. You can trust us. You're not alone anymore. We want to help but you have to let us."

I see a tear roll out from the corner of her eye and it trickles across her temple and into her hair. Ethan runs his palm across her forehead and his voice softens even more.

"Sky, honey, you did a great job all these years. Your parents would be so proud of you but do you really think they'd want you to have to do it all alone? There are a lot of bad people still left in the world to be fearful of but we aren't them. I'm a doctor and I've dedicated my life to helping people. Lance was a soldier and he protected people. Belle was a school teacher before the bombs. I hope you know that Rex and my son, Marshall are good people too. I know that Sasha did a horrible thing to you and your brother but she's just a mixed up kid and now that we're here we'll make sure she won't ever do anything like that again. We are the kind of people you can trust, I promise."

Sky reaches up to pull the mask off her face again. With a quick glance at the monitors, Ethan nods that she can. Her eyes are the saddest I've ever seen and her voice comes out in a broken croak.

"Most of you seem like good people but what about all the others? There are over a hundred people in here now. Do you really think I can trust all of them?" Her eyes glance back and forth between me and Ethan. I really don't know what to say. How can I reassure her when I don't even trust most of them myself? Thankfully, Ethan has the right words.

"Honey, you don't have to trust them. You just have to trust us. You put our group in charge of things over here and we will make sure it stays that way. We will protect you and Ben from any threats that might come up inside. There's no way we would jeopardize any of us or you and Ben. You took us into your home, Skylar. You're our family now."

Her eyes fill with tears and she tiredly shakes her head as her words come out in a slurred whisper. "I don't know what to do anymore."

I grip her hand tighter and Ethan smooths her hair back again before responding with a kind smile.

"You don't have to do anything right now except rest and get well. You're safe. Ben's safe. Just rest and we'll figure everything out when you're better."

Her eyes flutter closed and her hand goes limp in mine causing me to shoot Ethan a panicked look but he just smiles at me.

"It's ok Rex. I gave her a sedative in her IV and it's just fully taken hold. What Skylar needs more than anything right now is some peaceful rest. I'll stay here and watch over her. You should go and talk to her brother and let him know that she's going to be ok. Bring him back in a few hours so I can check him over but for right now it'd be better if he lets her rest."

I don't want to leave her again but I know he's right. Ben must be so scared for Sky by now. I'll take him and Matty over to tend to the animals to distract him for a while. I gently lay her hand back down on the bed before turning to go. I hope Ethan's words had an effect on her and once she's recovered we can start fresh. All I need is a chance.

Chapter Sixteen ... Skylar

I keep my eyes closed and listen to someone moving around near the bed I'm in. I think it's the doctor because I can hear the beeps of medical machines nearby. I don't know how long I've been here but I have vague memories of Benny and Rex both talking to me. What I do remember is facing off with Sasha, collapsing in the tunnel and Ethan's words about trust. I just don't know what to do with them.

The truth is, I'm tired. Not go to sleep tired but head and heart tired. I'm tired of replacing a real life with fantasies and dreams of one. I'm tired of everything being my responsibility. I'll never stop caring and protecting Ben but I'm tired of doing all the rest alone.

I let Dad's words echo in my mind again but they just don't have the same impact that they used too. He was right about so many things but he was wrong too. It was right to let the others into the barracks and he was right not to trust others, but not all others. Things are changing and not just here inside my home. I think the rain was the first step in the earth's healing. It might not be too long now before it's safe to live under the skies again. Dad used to talk about what we'd do once the skies cleared and it always involved finding other survivors to help and start rebuilding. So does it matter that they found me and Ben first? Aren't these the people we would have joined with to start rebuilding? I think they are.

I can't keep going the way I have been. Ethan was right, I did have a panic attack. I let my fear and mistrust overwhelm me to the point of collapse. That's not who I am or at least that's not who I've been before. I'm going to have to learn to deal with people again. It's fine to stay on guard but if Ben and I have any chance of being a part of the new world then I'm going to have to let go of the control I've clutched to my chest all these years. Starting with not pointing guns at people.

"What are you doing here?" I hear Ethan say. I keep my eyes closed because I'm still not ready to face others or if I'm honest, the embarrassment of my behavior. I haven't forgotten the way all those people looked at me last time they saw me.

“I…can I just sit here…please?”

The voice is female and I vaguely recognize it but can’t match a face to it. There’s a long pause before Ethan says, “Yes, I think maybe that would be a good idea.”

I hear the scrape of a chair beside my bed and then nothing. I try and just escape back into my thoughts but curiosity at who’s sitting there is nagging at me. After what feels like forever, I finally decide to open my eyes and see who it is when I hear something new. Whoever is sitting beside my bed is sniffling and I realize that they’re crying. Now I have to know who it is so I crack my eyes open a tiny bit but the surprise at who it is has my eyes popping wide open. I didn’t recognize the voice because I’ve only ever heard her speak in a sarcastic or scathing tone.

Sasha freezes in the act of wiping tears from her cheeks when she sees my eyes open and we just stare at each other for a minute. She finally moves and brushes away the dampness before looking away from me and down into her lap. Her breath hitches as she takes a deep breath before speaking.

“I…you…you almost died.”

I don’t know what she wants or what to say to her so I just shrug one shoulder. Her damp eyes flutter up to meet mine before quickly looking back down at her lap.

“I… didn’t want that. I… I’m sorry. I’m so sorry. I don’t know why I did those horrible things to you. I don’t know why I acted that way!”

The words rush out of her followed by a small sob. I still don’t know what to say so when she peeks up at me I give another shrug. This is all on her now. She has to be the one to say her peace.

“It’s not an excuse or at least not a good enough one, but, well, I was jealous. You’re so…and Rex is…arggg! I know now that you had things pretty bad too, just in a different way than we did. But, all I could see was this beautiful, clean, shiny girl in a perfect home with all the food and comfort that I lost and the one thing I thought I wanted was staring at you like I didn’t exist anymore. Rex, well, we grew up together and he is like my brother but for a while there, I let myself think that maybe it could be more than that. When I saw how he looked at you, I wanted to hurt you and nothing else seemed to matter. I've been sooo mad for so long at the world and at how unfair everything is that I just directed all of it at you."

Her eyes finally look up and lock on to mine before she continues.

"Skylar, I am so, so sorry for what I did and the way I treated you. I don't expect you to forgive me but I wanted you to know that."

Our eyes stay locked as I process her words and realize that this will have to be the first step I take if I want to move on. So I shrug again but this time I speak.

"This life sucks!"

Her eyes go wide but as she sees the small tired smile on my lips, she sobs out a half laugh. "Oh my God. It really does!"

It feels really good to just let that go right now so I try and lighten up some more.

"So, do you want to like, borrow each other's clothes now?"

She snorts out a laugh and is shaking her head but before she can reply to my small joke, the clinic's doors open and Marsh rushes in. His face is filled with determination when he spots Sasha and heads her way.

"I'd rather borrow your gun!" she says, glaring at him.

Marsh stumbles to a stop and a look of confusion crosses his face as he looks from Sasha's face to mine.

"Not gonna happen. I'm a better shot than you. I know just where to shoot him so he's only wounded and not dead." I say loud enough for him to hear. I remember every sexist word he said to us!

Marsh slowly raises his hands and starts to shuffle backward. Just as he reaches the door and is about to flee I call out in a hoarse voice.

"Hide your coconuts, Marsh, I'll be on my feet soon enough and there will be payback!"

Sasha bursts out laughing as Marsh high tails it out of the clinic but all I can manage is a weak smile. This little bit of activity has completely drained me and all I want now is to close my eyes.

Sasha must see it in my face because she gets up and gives my hand a squeeze before stepping away towards the door.

“Feel better soon, Skylar. I’ve got your crown all polished up for when you’re ready.”

As I slide back into the darkness I feel the smile form on my lips. That’s me, Queen of the apocalypse.

Chapter Seventeen ... Rex

I take a last look around Skylar and Ben's living quarters and nod in satisfaction. While Sky's been recuperating in the clinic, Matty, Ben and I have been putting in time cleaning up and tending to their garden and animals. I wanted to make sure that when Sky came back to her place she didn't have any work that needed to be done. It also helped keep mine and Ben's minds off worrying about her.

Ethan's told us both that he's happy with her recovery so far and after keeping her in the clinic for the past three days, says she should be ready to come home tomorrow. Ben's gotten a lot better too. He still needs to take it easy as he gets tired fast but he's having so much fun playing video games with Matty. Ben's been staying over in mine and Matty's room and between their late night whispers and my worrying about Sky I haven't had a good night's sleep in over a week. I hope that will change tonight. I've popped in now and then to check on Sky but mainly left her alone to recover. Now that Ethan's ready to let her come home I think she's well enough to have a real conversation about all that's happened and what our future holds.

"All right boys, wrap it up. Dinner should be ready over in the barracks soon."

Ben and Matty groan about shutting down the game they're playing but shut it off anyways. We take our time walking back through the tunnel so that Ben can keep up. Ethan's told me that walking around is good for Ben's lungs but to take it slow for the next week. The boys chatter about what they think will be for dinner and even after being inside for a week, I still can't get used to the abundance of food available to us now.

Our group had eaten better than the hotel people but none of us have had any extra weight on our bodies from rationing for so long. It fills my heart to see Matty's cheeks start to fill out a bit and he looks so much healthier than before. Everyone that Skylar let in looks better. It's amazing what enough good food, heat, hot water and safety can do for people. I know that none of us will ever take it for granted now that we have a second chance at having it all.

As we head towards the tables that are full of happy chatting people, I smile. For the first few days, people would stay silent and stare down at their plates while eating quickly like they thought the food would magically disappear. Now, everyone is more relaxed and there's conversation and laughter at every meal.

The boys and I slide into spots around Marsh and Lance and dig in to the platter of roast beef and mashed potatoes. I know the potatoes are made from flakes and they're not as good as the fresh ones from Skylar's garden but the gravy poured on top of them makes them almost as good. My favorite part of the meals now are no sprouts. Dehydrated veggies are far from yummy but I'll take them over the daily serving of sprouts we were forced to eat for the last seven years.

I look up from my plate when I catch sight of more people joining our group and see Sasha and Belle start filling their plates. I send Belle a smile and nod of thanks for another amazing meal but only give Sasha a cool nod. Marsh and Ethan have both told me that she and Skylar have talked and seemed to have gotten past what Sasha did but I'm not quite ready to forgive her so easily. It's going to take a long time before I forget her betrayal of Matty and me.

I rush through dinner and leave the boys in Lance and Marsh's care before jogging over to the clinic. I've had days to think of the words I want to say to Sky once she was well enough for us to talk but I'm still not sure how she'll respond. When I get to the doors to the clinic, I peek through the window and see Ethan and Sky are eating dinner together. Sky's propped up in bed with a tray in front of her and Ethan's sitting beside her with a plate balanced on his lap. They seem to be in deep conversation so I step back from the door and lean against the wall.

I know Ethan's been talking to Skylar a lot about everything she's had to deal with since her parents died. I hope he's been able to help her work through some of her pain. I still can't imagine how hard it would have been to grow up all alone and be a parent to Ben at the same time. I don't know if I would have been able to do it without Belle, Ethan, and Lance filling in as parents for Matty and me after our Mom died. Not to mention having Marsh as my best friend. Sky hasn't even had a friend to unload on except AIRIA.

"Rex, are you going to stand guard out here all night or are going to go in and talk to her?"

I'm so deep in thought that I don't even hear Ethan come out of the clinic and his words have me jumping away from the wall.

"Oh! Hey, Ethan. How's she doing?"

He puts a hand on my shoulder and laughs. "She doing great but she'd be a lot better if you had a real conversation with her. She thinks you're mad at her for what happened with Sasha before she collapsed." He laughs again at my startled expression. "Rex, more than anything, she needs to be reassured by you. She's been through a lot and we've talked through most of it but I can't be the one to tell her that the boy she likes still likes her back."

I glance over at the doors and then back at him. "She…she's really worried I don't like her anymore? How can she think that? I'm the reason all this bad stuff happened to her and Ben! If anything she should be mad at me!"

My face changes to a scowl as Ethan starts to laugh at me again. "Rex, just go talk to her!" He's still chuckling as he turns and walks away but not before I hear him say something about "young love".

I take another look in the window at Sky and see her with her head back and eyes closed. I take a deep breath and slowly push through the doors. Her eyes stay closed as I settle silently down into the chair that Ethan had just vacated. Her face is still very pale with dark circles under her eyes and the angry red blisters from the rain are now a lighter shade. Her hair has lost some of its golden shine but she's still the most beautiful girl I've ever seen.

She must feel me staring at her because her eyes slowly open. She gives me a tentative smile and her hand trembles slightly when she lifts it from the bed to offer it to me. I take her hand and bring it to my lips for a kiss before meeting her eyes and saying,

"I'm so sorry Sky. Everything that happened to you and Ben is all my fault. Can you forgive me?"

Her eyes go wide in surprise and she starts shaking her head.

“No, no Rex! How can you say that? You had no control over what happened! Sasha and Ted made their own choices. You had no control over any of it!” She squeezes my hand tighter and pulls me closer. “Listen, Rex. I made a choice to save you and Matty that day and bring you inside. It was the right thing to do. I’ve spent the last seven years hiding from the world and even though I questioned everything my Dad told me, I never did anything to try and help others. I did the right thing when I helped you and it was also the right thing to let all those people in here. No one’s to blame for Ben and me getting sick except maybe me for not following up on decontamination procedures.” She lets out a deep sigh and drops her eyes. “I’ve made a lot of mistakes since we met but letting you into my life wasn’t one of them. I’m sorry for the way I’ve been acting since then.”

My admiration for her surges even higher. After everything that’s happened, she’s giving us another chance to be a part of her life. I hope that includes more for both of us.

“Um, do you think…would you want to…when you feel better, would you want to go on a date with me?” I manage to stutter out. I feel my face flame up in embarrassment at my inept attempt to ask her out but feel relief when her smile splits across her face.

“Wow, I’ve never been on a date before, Rex. I would love that! Where should we go? Out for dinner and a movie?” she teases.

I give her a smug smile. “Actually, yes, that’s exactly what I had in mind.” I have to laugh at her confused, disbelieving expression. “The dinner part of the evening would take place at Chez Rex. It’s a new bistro that will be open for one night of magical dining. We would follow that at the Barrack’s cinema that runs featured films twice a week on the newly installed projector and back wall. It’s the talk of the town and seats are highly coveted!”

Her eyes are dancing with delight and she gives me a serious nod. “Well, how can a girl say no to that? I would be honored to attend with you!”

We sit and talk about all the things we want to see happen in the future until her eyes start to droop. The smile never leaves my face and her hand stays in mine until she drifts off to sleep.

Chapter Eighteen ... Skylar

It's good to be home. Everything is in its place and Ben's at the table grumbling through his school work for the first time since we got sick. Ethan's cautioned me to take it easy for the next few weeks but after being stuck in a bed for the last eight days, I'm ready to get back into my routine. The only problem is my legs are still a little wobbly and the old routine doesn't feel quite right anymore.

I used to spend my days helping Ben with school work and doing chores in the cavern. The animals and garden still need daily work but the canning, drying and freezing of all the extra food that I used to do seems silly when there are people next door that could benefit from it in its fresh state.

I leave Ben to his work and wander slowly out into the cavern and into the storage rooms. I see all the extra supplies with new eyes now. I no longer look at what we have for just two people but how it can be shared out to over a hundred. AIRIA has a running inventory of all that was here to start and all that we've both used and added to it over the years. I'm sure if I asked, she could tell me exactly how long everything here and in the barracks storage would last with so many people but I'd rather not know right now. Instead, I think about how to produce more.

I know they've started their gardens on the other side but if we add clippings and shoots from my garden, we could move things along faster. The small flock of chickens I have can easily be increased until there's enough to give everyone fresh eggs. The fish in my small cavern stream can be increased as well.

The weirdest thing I learned while talking to Ethan while I was stuck in the clinic is that my cow, Nodds can be inseminated to make a baby cow. Apparently, there is frozen "stuff" to make that happen over in the clinic. Ethan was pretty excited about that and the other frozen "stuff" they have over there. I'm more than happy to leave all that in his hands to deal with.

With bigger gardens and more animals producing food, we won't be as dependent on the food stored and it will last even longer. At some point, we will all need to talk about the bigger future of living outside again but until we get some kind of forecast from AIRIA, I'm not sure when that will be.

I check on Ben and let him know I'm going over to the other side. He whines and grumbles but he resigns himself to getting caught up on his schoolwork when I don't budge. Especially after I promise him time with Matty after he's done.

As I slowly make my way down the tunnel to the other side, I think about putting together some kind of school for the kids. I don't know exactly how many kids are over in the barracks but it might be a good idea to get them all together. I think of all the things AIRIA taught Dad and me in the first two years we lived in the bunker and realise that we should have classes for everyone to learn about agriculture. We'll need all the knowledge we can get once we start rebuilding outside.

When I get to the end of the tunnel, I stop and practice the breathing exercises Ethan has taught me. He really helped me understand why I was having panic attacks. Being around so many people after years of being alone with just Ben as well as the fear Dad instilled in me of others combined to give me a phobia that I need to work through and learn to control. I seem to be ok with just a few people around but in groups of more than four, I start to get overwhelmed. I need to get it under control because I plan on working with all of these people from now on and I refuse to be weak.

"AIRIA, where is Belle located?"

"Skylar Ross, Belle last name unknown is currently located in the private Officer's living quarters."

I take one last calming breath before swiping open the door. As much as I plan to overcome this dumb phobia, I'm relieved that I won't have to go out into the main barracks where most of the group is. Small steps!

I walk through the offices and can't help but peek into open doors as I go by. Where once there were rooms filled with desks and computer equipment, there are now bunks instead. I quicken my pace when a few people glance up at me as I go by. I still haven't interacted with any of them and I know they probably don't have a very good opinion of me after the way I acted when I let them in or when I was sick. I'm just not ready to talk to anyone I haven't met yet. Approaching Belle will be my first step.

I finally come to the officer's suites and start looking in the open doors for Belle. When I hear female voices, I skip the rest and head to the door they're coming from. Inside, I see Belle and Sasha standing in front of a mirror. Sasha's frowning at her reflection as she tugs on the plain uniform shirt she's wearing.

"We can try and take it in a bit to make it more flattering but unfortunately it's all we have to work with. I've looked through all the storage rooms and the only fabric there are the same materials these clothes are made of. I'm sorry we left all our bags outside but it's not like we had a choice once the rain started." Belle said.

Sasha yanks her tucked shirt out of her pants and ties the tails in a knot before shaking her head. "It's ok, Mom. It's not that big a deal. I just wish we had something a little different. I kinda feel like a clone with all of us wearing the exact same thing."

"I can help."

The words are out of my mouth before I realize they might not appreciate me eavesdropping on their conversation. They both jump and spin around.

"Sorry, I was looking for you, Belle, and the door was open and I overheard your conversation. I…" I stop talking as Belle strides towards me with a warm smile.

"Skylar! It's so good to see you up and around. I don't think we've been properly introduced. How are you feeling?"

I'm a bit taken back by her warm greeting. I wasn't sure how she'd react to me after what happened between her daughter and me but I wasn't expecting this. I take the hand she offers and shake it while looking over her shoulder at Sasha, who just looks back with a neutral expression.

"Please, come in! You should sit down. Ethan's said you will need to rest for a while until you're back to full strength."

I let her guide me to the small couch and sit. I'm not sure how I feel about everyone knowing my medical condition but I guess it doesn't really matter.

"Um, I was just coming to talk to you about my garden and a few other things but I heard uh, I mean, I have different fabric!"

Belle gives me a patient smile at my stuttering and waves Sasha over. When she takes a chair across from me her Mom settles beside me on the couch and takes my hand.

"I know you and Sasha have had a chance to talk but I wanted to tell you myself just how grateful I am to you for letting us all into your home and how generous you've been with sharing all your supplies. I know that there were some bad things that happened to you and your brother because of that. I just wanted you to know that both Sasha and I are sorry for everything and we hope that we can put it all behind us."

I have to look away from this kind woman. She's not only forgiven me for pointing a gun at her daughter's head but she reminds me of my own mother. I have to gulp back the tears that flood my throat before I can reply. I shoot a quick look at Sasha but she's looking at her own lap.

"I…well, none of us were at our best in the last few weeks. I certainly made my own mistakes too. I, um, I would like to put it behind us too."

Belle squeezes my hand and gives me such a compassionate look that I almost turn into a quivering piece of jello right then and there. I can't believe how nice this woman is. I clear my throat and change the subject before I crawl into her lap and bawl like a baby.

"So, I have different fabric in my storage rooms. My Dad stocked up on stuff he thought my…mom…and I would like." My voice hitches on the word mom but I keep going. "I would be happy to share it with you. I have a few sewing machines too but I know there are more over here in storage. AIRIA has clothing patterns in her database you could use to make different clothes."

Sasha's head shoots up and her eyes are filled with excitement. I can't really blame her. It wasn't very long ago that I was dreaming of fancy prom dresses. I learned a long time ago to make new clothes for me and Ben. Sasha sends a questioning look to her Mom who nods back.

"That would be very welcome Skylar. It's not that we don't appreciate the new clean clothes over here, it's just that they aren't very…"

"Pretty?" I finish for her.

Sasha snorts, “Ha, understatement!”

We all share a laugh before Belle turns back to me.

“What did you want to talk to me about, besides fashion styles?”

“Oh, right. Well, Rex told me that you were in charge of the garden before so I thought you might be interested in looking mine over. I know you guys have planted yours over here but I have a lot growing that you could take shoots and clippings from to speed up production over here.

"Also, Ethan told me you were a teacher before, so I thought you might have some ideas about setting up a school for the younger kids. I have lots of textbooks and AIRIA has even more information in her data banks to help with that. Ben’s doing pretty well with his school work but it would be really nice if he could have a few classes with other kids. Except for Matty just recently, he’s never even seen other children so I think it’d be good for him.

"I was also thinking it would be helpful to start running adult classes on things we need to know to start rebuilding once we can move back outside. I don’t know when that will happen but we should start preparing for it. I think…what? I’m sorry. Did I say something wrong?”

I look back and forth from Sasha and Belle and feel my face falling at their dropped open mouths. I guess I’m overstepping with my ideas and I’m about to bolt from the room when Belle leans over and gives me a huge hug. I’m so confused but a look at Sasha over her mom’s shoulder doesn’t help me understand what’s happening here. She’s just shaking her head in amazement. Belle leans back away from me and starts to laugh at my expression.

“Wow! Just, wow and YES, to all of it! Skylar, just yes!” She’s still laughing so I again look to Sasha who throws up her hands.

“Well hold on a minute. I need to replace your crown with a halo now! Seriously, what are you, a saint?”

I feel myself start to relax at her teasing tone and look to Belle who is nodding her head. “Let’s start with taking a look at your garden and then we’ll go from there.”

As we get up to go over to my area, I feel something inside I haven't felt in a long time. Hope. Hope for a real future where Ben and I won't be alone.

Chapter Nineteen ... Rex

Sky's been on her feet for a week now and every day I see improvement in both her health and her mental state as she spends more and more time with us in the barracks. She still stays on the edge of any big groups but I've seen her talking with more and more of the people from the hotel as we work to set up her classroom idea. She seems to be the most comfortable with people who have kids that will be attending the half day school.

She's thrown herself into helping to get the barracks set up to run as smooth as her side of the cave. She's so full of ideas and suggestions that the people are turning to her more and more for her leadership capabilities and we haven't had much one on one time. I'm ok with that because I'm usually right by her side to do the heavy lifting. Ethan's insisting she take her physical limitations seriously or she might have a setback.

We've spent the day together working on transplanting shoots and cuttings from Sky's garden to the barracks and we're both grimy from the soil we've been digging in all day.

"Do you think there's time for a shower before the meeting?" she asks as we head towards the offices.

"I'd love to say yes to that but look, there are Ethan and Belle heading towards the offices now. She probably had to drag him out of the clinic for the meeting so let's get in there before he escapes! We can stop at my place and just wash off the worst of it."

Sky grumbles but picks up her pace. We get most of the black dirt cleaned off of our arms before joining the rest of the group in one of the boardrooms for our first official planning meeting. Seated around the table are Lance, Ethan, Belle, Sasha, Marsh and two people from the hotel group. The man is Gordon Hawksbill who has forty years of farming experience and Lana Bottle who had worked in one of the country's biggest greenhouse farms before she was stranded in Canmore the day the bombs dropped. They have both been running things in the grow areas since we came inside.

I take a seat beside Marsh and steal half the mound of cookies he has on a napkin in front of him. I could have just taken some from the serving platter in the middle of the table but it's more fun to see him bite back the complaint he's ready to voice when Skylar skews him with a pointed look. I'm having a blast with the way Marsh has been acting around Skylar since he joined the land of the cave man with his sexist comments to her and Sasha, even if it did defuse the situation. If I didn't know him as well as I do, I'd swear he was scared of her. Before I can take a verbal jab at him, Lance starts talking.

"All right everyone, this will hopefully be the first of many planning sessions for the future of our group. We will go over how things are going here inside and what plans we want to change or implement in the days to come as well as get some information on what's happening outside and what plans we want to start thinking about for the future.

"The kind generosity of Skylar sharing her supplies has allowed everyone to start on the road to better health but it's very important that we look towards self-sufficiency rather than just live off of the supplies until they're exhausted. We also need to keep a reserve of stored food for when the time comes for us to move out into the world. So, first thing is, let's find out what's happening out there.

"AIRIA, can you give us a report on the weather conditions outside and any forecast you have access to? Can you predict when the rain will stop?"

"Lance Malone, current conditions are intermittent rain showers. Precipitation has not been continuous since it started and it is becoming less frequent. Last satellite connection has shown that the eastern part of the country has clear skies and warming temperatures of five degrees lower than pre- bombing seasonal levels. Historical forecast trends predict that the western region of this area will follow similar trends."

There is silence around the table as we all process what that means. The skies have cleared in the east and temperatures have risen. The earth is healing. Lance looks from all our faces before asking the computer his next question.

"AIRIA, what about the radiation and acid rain?"

"Lance Malone, radiation continues at high levels in direct hit locations. Residual radiation will be a concern in top soil and standing vegetation and possibly metal structures."

"The chemicals in precipitation would have lessened with every rainfall and should have cleared by this time."

"AIRIA, what recommendation are there for clearing away residual radiation so that crops can be grown safely?"

"Lance Malone, it is recommended that controlled burns are used to clear all areas of future crop locations and six to twelve inches of top soil should be removed. Tests can be performed to determine if ground contaminants are still present."

Lance leans back into his chair and rubs at his chin in thought before looking to Gordon. The man is already shaking his head.

"Years, it would take years to clear enough land by hand to sustain us all through one winter. Even if every person we have here went to work with a shovel on one field, it would take at least a year to clear it, plow it and remove that much top soil. The next year we would have to plow it again and then seed it and hope for a harvest that would sustain half of our numbers. I'm pretty confident that the growing season won't be as long as it used to be so that's a consideration too. Having to do it all by hand will take years."

At his words, everyone's faces fall. The news that the skies are clearing had given us all hope that we might be able to start rebuilding soon. After seven years of barely surviving, it has been amazing to have the comforts of the bunker but each and every one of us has a huge desire to start building a future out under the sun. It will happen but it will take a very long time and a huge commitment from every person left alive to make it happen.

Sky leans forward and raises her hand to ask a question. At Lance's nod, she turns to Gordon to address him.

"How long would it take if you had machinery?"

He scoffs before answering.

"One tractor and enough fuel would see us having a harvest that might feed us all through a long winter in one season but I heard that the tractor store and the gas station both went out of business!"

Sky ignores his sarcasm and just nods.

"AIRIA, what's in storage on the second level?"

"Skylar Ross, do you wish a detailed inventory or just the basics?"

Skylar rolls her eyes at the ceiling before saying,

"Just the basics, AIRIA!"

"Skylar Ross, second underground level storage mainly contains mechanical equipment and gas storage."

At Gordon's disbelieving expression, Skylar starts to grin and nod.

"AIRIA, would that include farm machinery?"

"Skylar Ross, yes it does."

Chapter Twenty ... Skylar

The room erupts with overjoyed conversation at AIRIA's words. I knew there was a lot of machinery on the lower level but I had no idea what most of it was used for. I can't help but grin at how happy everyone is and at the thought of being able to rebuild so much faster with all the supplies available to us.

The man across from me with all the farming experience is shaking his head in disbelief. He leans forward to be heard and booms out his question at me.

"Young lady, how exactly did you come to be in the possession of all of this? The bunker, the supplies, this magic computer?"

The smile dims on my face at the reminder that the people who put me here are gone but I push past it to answer his question. Everyone turns their eyes to me to hear my answer and Rex reaches for my hand.

"My father was a soldier in the military. One of his best friends and my godfather is…was a high-ranking general. When my dad first started to get serious about prepping for a major disaster, he looked at buying property out here in the mountains. When my Uncle Bill came for a visit, Dad brought him out for his thoughts on this area. I didn't find out until after the bombs that Uncle Bill bought the land and had the bunkers built and stocked. Apparently, there is a twin to this bunker somewhere in the east. Dad said that this one was off the books, whatever that means."

Lance holds up his hand to stop any more questions and turns to me with an alarmed face.

"This place belongs to the government? Where have they been for the last seven years?"

I shrug my shoulders. "Don't know. Dad said hardly anyone knew about this place. Uncle Bill kept it to himself, Dad and a select few in his inner circle. Dad said it was a backup in case things went bad in the east. So, after seven years, I'd say no one's coming."

Lance relaxes and starts to nod. "I'm going to agree with that but, with the east already having clear skies, we might end up being noticed out here. I would suggest that it's easier to ask for forgiveness than permission. We should get moving on plans like where we are going to start rebuilding and then get as much of the machinery and supplies moved to that location. If anyone from the east does show up, well, it'll be a done deal."

I lean back and let the talk flow over me as AIRIA brings up a detailed map of the province on the large screen against one wall and people move from their chairs to get a better look.

I try and picture what life will be like living outside. As much as I crave open skies and the sun on my face, it will also mean letting go of a lot of things. Things like my home and the security and comfort its given Ben and me all these years. The other thing I'd have to give up is AIRIA. The thought makes me nauseous. She might just be a computer, but to me, she's been a lifeline to sanity. After dad died, she was the only thing I had left of him. She answered all my questions as I tried to figure out growing up and parenting at the same time. She might not be a real person but to me, she was the closest thing I had to a parent. I'm not sure I'm ready to walk away from that.

"Hey, you ok in there? You look like you're a million miles away." Rex nudges me.

My eyes refocus on what's happening in the room and I see everyone settling back into their seats. I send him a reassuring smile and focus back into the conversation just as Lance asks me a question.

"Skylar, how do you feel about us having a detailed inventory printed out? It would make planning a lot easier if we knew exactly what was available to us but I want you to be comfortable with that."

Before I have a chance to say "no problem", Gordon speaks up.

"Why does it matter what she thinks? Technically, none of this stuff belongs to her. From what she said, it was our tax dollars that built and supplied all of this so it belongs to all of us!"

My whole body goes stiff with tension at the tone he's using but its Lance that responds with a hand slammed on the table. His face is cold and hard when he slowly rises from his seat and leans over the table in Gordon's direction. The tone of his voice is so hard that it sends shivers down my spine.

"Technically, the water and shelter of the hotel belonged to everyone but you cowed under Ted's malicious rule for seven years without doing a thing about it. Technically, I didn't have to save your ass and bring you or anyone else with my group but I did. Technically, Skylar didn't have to let you or any of us in but she did. Technically, she didn't have to offer all of the supplies to us or the supplies we will need to rebuild but she has. So in my books, that girl is BOSS of everything in here and if you can't get on board and deliver the respect she deserves then you technically, shouldn't be a part of any future plans. DO YOU UNDERSTAND?"

He doesn't yell the last three words but he puts so much force behind them that he might as well have.

Gordon's shoulders are pinned back against his seat as he tries to get away from the forcefulness of Lance's words. He starts nodding his head in agreement but only manages to squeak out, "Yes, of course."

There's such a deep silence in the room after that I want to just jump up and bolt but Rex's hand in mine gives me the courage to stay and speak.

"AIRIA, please print out a detailed inventory of all storage contents."

"Skylar Ross, printing now."

We all can hear the sound of a printer clicking on in the next room as it starts to spit out sheet after sheet of what we have to work with. It's Belle that finally breaks the silence.

"I think we should table our expansion plans for now and move on to what's happening inside." When she gets relieved nods all around the table she continues.

"Honestly, everything is going amazingly well! Everyone has made themselves available for shifts in maintenance, gardening and cooking.

"The garden received a boost over the last few days as we added shoots and cuttings from Skylar's garden. We should see some yield within the next few weeks.

"Ethan has added the animals to his duties and is working on increasing the headcount there.

"We've started up the school sessions for the children but decided to make it half day. We thought it was just as important for them to sit in on the adult agriculture classes as well. We will all need to gain as much knowledge from AIRIA as we can before we leave here.

"So, with everything going so well, some of us thought we should have a party to celebrate."

Sasha is practically vibrating in her seat at her mom's words and I have to admit the idea of that sounds kind of exciting but Lance must not feel the same because he's already shaking his head.

"A party, really? Is that something we really need to be focusing on?"

I smother the laugh that wants to come out when Ethan stretches out his arm and lightly clotheslines Lance forcing him back into his seat.

"Ignore him, Belle. What do you have in mind?"

She's grinning at his antics when she explains.

"There hasn't been a whole lot to celebrate for the last seven years with most of the people barely surviving. We now have a safe shelter with enough food to start healing our bodies. Top that with the sky clearing and the weather shifting so we can start planning for a real future and it deserves a…thanksgiving."

Lance is still shaking his head but a small smile is tugging on his lips when he says, "It's April, wrong month for that!"

But he waves her on when Ethan jabs him in the ribs.

Belle ignores him and keeps going. "No matter what month it is, I think we all have a lot to celebrate and be thankful for. Just the fact that we managed to survive the end of civilization as we knew it and can now start planning for a real future is enough to celebrate. I think it would be good for everyone's morale.

"So, as I was saying, we could have a feast followed by a dance." She looks around the table and her smile gets even wider at all of the nods and "yesses" sent her way. "Excellent! Let's say three days from now. That will give us time to plan and organize it and make a few dresses."

Lance shoots to his feet and points at Belle with a mock stern look.

"Aha! There's the real reason right there! You girls just want an excuse to get dressed up!"

The meeting ended there with laughter and chatter about the party ideas. I catch Sasha's eyes and we both break out laughing at the pure glee in each other's eyes. It might not be the prom but it's the closest either one of us will ever come to, so we're both going to make the most of it.

Chapter Twenty-One ... Rex

I don't understand girls. Seriously, flat out don't understand. Not that long ago, Skylar and Sasha were total enemies and now they're almost inseparable, giggling and gushing over fabric and patterns for dresses. I just ran far, far away when they started talking about hairstyles. I'm not sure what happened to the gun wielding bad ass girl that I fell for but I will say that it's nice to see her so happy.

Belle is a whirlwind of activity and she doesn't hold back making Marsh and me do her grunt work. While she organizes food preparation and recipes as well as lining up women who are proficient with sewing machines to add more variety to their wardrobes, Marsh and I are stuck with decorating. The empty space that was created in the middle of the barracks when all the bunks were moved around will be our dance floor. Skylar dug out all the Christmas decorations she had on her side and left the boxes for Marsh and me to sort through. I don't think I've ever seen so much glitter in my life. We're both completely clueless when it comes to decorating so when we found the huge tangle of twinkle lights we called it good and just strung them up all around the dance floor.

After congratulating ourselves on a job well done we head to the kitchen to find a well-deserved snack. The place is organized chaos as they put together the feast and the smells are amazing. Belle spots us and starts to wave us out but there's no way we're leaving without a taste of something.

"Fine, there's some spaghetti left from last night that I can warm up for you guys but keep your fingers out of the rest! How's the decorating coming?" Belle asks as we follow her to a quieter area of the massive kitchen.

"Done," Marsh announces proudly.

I nod in agreement when she squints her eyes in disbelief. When she just keeps me pinned with her stare, I elaborate.

"Really, we put up a bunch of little Christmas lights all around where you want the dance floor to be!"

"Annnnnd?" she prompts.

Marsh and I look at each other in confusion before he shrugs.

"And what? It's done. It should look rad if we turn the overhead lights down."

She puts her hands on her hips and we both take a step back. After seven years we know when Belle's about to blast us.

"Out of all of those boxes of decorations Skylar gave you, all you could come up with was a few strings of lights? After all these years together, how many birthdays and Christmases have you seen me decorate our space to try and make things special for you all? Even when we were barely hanging on, I still managed to spruce our space up to make it look like a party! Here you are with almost unlimited supplies to make things beautiful for our celebration and all you do is put up some lights? Is that what you're telling me?"

Marsh is looking around for an escape route so I take the hit for us.

"No, no Belle! That's just the start. Uh, we knew the lights had to go up first so we got that done and then we, uh, got hungry so we thought we'd get a snack before finishing up with the rest. You'll see, it'll be the best-decorated party ever, promise!"

Belle gives up the steely eye that has a glint of amusement in it before finally relenting.

"Well then, I guess I'd better get you hard workers some food so you can get back at it."

As soon as she turns her back to the fridge, Marsh pretends to throttle me before throwing his hands up in a "What are going to do now" gesture. I just shrug my shoulders and plaster a fake smile on my face when Belle turns and hands us both plates of cold spaghetti.

"You don't need these warmed up, do you? I figure you're both anxious to get back to work," she says with a smirk and a sharp eye towards Marsh.

"Nope, no this is great Belle. Thanks for the grub. We'll just take it out into the barracks and get out of your way!" he says cheerfully before snatching the plate and making a beeline for the door.

When I finally catch up with him, he's already halfway through his cold food and I get a glare.

"What the heck, Dude? Since when did you turn into that Martha, uh, housekeeping superwoman?"

"I'm not! But how're we supposed to say no to her when she's right? Don't you remember how she had Lance and Ethan scavenging attics and basements all over town for holiday decorations? She did that for us, man. We might not have gotten a pile of new toys but she made sure we all had a special day for holidays. We owe her! Besides, when she gets that hands on the hips thing going on, well it just, I mean she's so…"

Marsh's shoulders slump when he finishes my sentence. "Like a mom." At my grateful smile and nod, he waves at my plate. "Alright Martha, shovel it down and let's go prettify the place."

Chapter Twenty-Two ... Skylar

"Oh, Mom!" Sasha breathes out in a soft gasp of wonder when she gets her first look at her finished hair.

I smile in admiration at the soft beautiful red curls that cascade down her back. This day so far has been so much fun and we still have a few hours to go before the feast and dance starts. The teenage girl in me has surfaced in spades and I'm loving every minute of the ritual that I never got to do with my own mom.

We've spent the last three days sewing patterns for skirts and dresses along with some of the other ladies in the barracks so that everyone who wants too will have something different to wear for the party. I glance at the dress I'll be wearing that's hanging from the back of the door on a hanger and sigh. It's the only one that wasn't made from scratch. The day the bombs dropped, my Mom and I had grabbed what we could from our home in the city but dresses weren't high on the list. The only dress my mother brought was a flowing maternity dress that was an empire cut. Belle had helped me take it apart and refit it to my much slimmer build.

I can't help but run my hand down the soft, shiny yellow material. I feel my eyes mist as I remember Mom wearing it and how it reminds me of sunshine and love. She might not be here with me today for my first dance but I'm sure she will be in my heart as I wear her dress.

I turn back to Sasha and Belle and see Belle's eyes are misty too. Her gaze meets mine and she shakes her head and laughs.

"Such a silly thing when so much is more important but oh how I've missed a good curling iron! Skylar, I think your mother would be very pleased that you've shared her things with us girls."

I nod in agreement. "Me too. Honestly, I forgot that she had brought some of this stuff with her. Dad had put all her things away after…after she died."

Sasha tosses her newly curled hair over her shoulder as she studies her reflection in the mirror. "I'm thankful too. I didn't know my hair could look like this!" She turns away from the mirror to face me. "You wouldn't happen to have any makeup or jewelry would you?" she glances over to her mom. "We had some stuff but it was left outside when the rain started."

I shake my head wistfully. If there was makeup, Dad must have thrown it out. The only jewellery I have is Mom and Dad's wedding rings. "No, I couldn't find anything else. It's too bad, I've always wanted to try mascara. My eyelashes are so blond they barely show up!" We all laugh and talk about girly things that we haven't had room for in our lives for so long. It's so nice to be with other females and talk about such silly things.

Belle starts taking out the braids she wove into my damp hair to create rippling waves for a fancier hairstyle.

"Sasha, can you run over and check on things in the kitchen for me while I do Skylar's hair? I'm sure it's all on track but I want things to be perfect for tonight. Tell the boys I said to start getting cleaned up and ready too. Once you're back, it should be just about time to get changed into our dresses and we can all head over together."

Sasha has a thoughtful look on her face but she finally nods and with a grin dashes off. I sit patiently as Belle uses small scissors to snip away at the blunt bangs I had chopped into my hair when I cut out the burnt pieces after we were caught out in the rain. I'm so excited to see what she's doing. I've never given any thought to my hair or a style unless it was to get it out of my face. All of this is so new and exciting for me.

I can't wait for the party and to see how everyone looks. Belle told me she had forced haircuts on all the boys this morning and I smile as I remember the griping and complaining I had heard from Ben and Matty when they came in to play a few video games. There was even more complaining from the two of them when we kicked them out so we could have our makeovers. I finally relented and let them take the gaming console over to the other side so they could keep playing.

When I had decided to finally trust Rex's group and start integrating both sides of the bunker, I had AIRIA upgrade the authorization for Lance, Ethan, Belle, Sasha and the boys. It just didn't make sense to only let Rex move back and forth freely through the tunnel. I'm still not ready to give such access to the rest of the people over there but his group can now cross over whenever they need too.

"Did you finish the sandals?" Belle asks, breaking me out of my thoughts.

"Oh, I did! They look so pretty!" The day we came here, it was summer and Mom was wearing a pair of plain black sandals. Other than tough and heavy hiking and work boots stocked in storage, I only had my running shoes to wear. When I sorted through Mom's belongings that Dad had saved, I found the sandals and thought they would work better with the dress. I had taken some of the yellow fabric we had cut out of the dress and used it to wrap around the black bands on the sandals to match the dress.

"Well good because your hair is done and I want to see the whole package so why don't you slip on your dress and shoes and we can see the final effect!"

I want nothing more than to look at what she's done to my hair but I know it will be more fun to see the completed look so I keep my head turned from the mirror and grab my dress from the hanger. Belle steps out so I can change and I'm practically vibrating with excitement as I let the dress fall over my head and strap on the matching sandals. Before I turn to look in the mirror, I lift my head up to the ceiling and close my eyes.

"Mom, Dad, I hope you're there and I hope you're both watching down on me and Ben. I know you didn't want me to trust anyone, Dad, but today for the first time I actually feel like I'm seventeen and I think that's ok. I'll still take care of Ben and keep him safe but today, today's for me…ok?"

I almost choke with tears when the speaker above me comes to life.

"So proud of you, Sky."

Mom's soft voice floats down before it cuts to Dad saying,

"You're my best girl, Sky."

For a computer, AIRIA sure knows right what's needed and when. AIRIA might be nothing more than cold circuit boards but I love her and I don't know what I'd do without her.

"Thank you, AIRIA."

"Skylar Ross, it is my pleasure."

I take a deep breath and turn slowly to look at my transformed self in the mirror. What I see, takes my breath away. It's like looking at a ray of sunshine. My blond hair is golden ripples with yellow fabric ribbons threaded through it. The summer dress has wide straps that connect to a bodice that tightens just under my chest. The rest of the dress flows out from there and reaches just past my knees. I twist my hips in a quick motion and see the skirt flare out beautifully making me laugh in delight. This isn't the prom dress of my dreams, it's better.

I bounce in the cute redesigned sandals and then rush out the door to show Belle. She steps out of the bathroom at almost the same time and her face says it all. I can't help but admire the change in her as well. Her deep red hair that matches her daughters has been curled and swept up high on her head so that only a few loose curls float down to touch her shoulders. She looks so much younger than I thought she was.

We both stand there beaming at each other like idiots until the door to the cavern slides open and Ben comes barreling through. He's already calling out to me before he's made it halfway through the door.

"Sky, I wanna…."

He skids to a stop and his mouth drops open in shock. An amazed whisper gushes from his small mouth.

"Sky, you look like a princess!"

I can't help the huge grin that spreads across my face at his reaction to my makeover.

"Thank you, Ben. You look pretty handsome too with your new haircut!"

His expression changes from grin to scowl at that reminder and his little hands go to his hips.

"Sky, I wanna go outside!"

I spurt out a laugh at the unexpected demand making his scowl deepen.

"It's not fair! I've never been outside in my whole life. That's like, **forever**! I've only seen pictures and TV outside. I wanna go see the real outside!"

I step over to him shaking my head in amusement of his dramatic seven years of forever life and put my hands on his shoulders.

"Ben, I will take you outside. I promise! We just need to wait for the weather to clear and for it to be safe. Someday soon, all of us will be living outside!"

He shakes his head and stomps his foot in frustration.

"I want to go now not someday! It's not fair! How come Rex and Sasha can go now but I can't?" He whines.

I look from Ben's face over to Belle's in confusion but her face has gone white and she beats me too it.

"What do you mean, Ben? What are Rex and Sasha doing?" She asks him in a panicked voice.

Ben's scowl turns to an expression of worry and hesitation at her tone and he looks down at his shoes. I'm still holding his shoulders so I give him a tiny shake, my own concern creeping up on me.

"Ben! What are Rex and Sasha doing?"

He keeps his eyes down but his voice is filled with guilt. "It was supposed to be a surprise for you."

My heart speeds up and I'm starting to feel scared but I don't know why so I put all the calm I can into my voice and ask again.

"What are they doing?"

His eyes peek up at me, "They went outside to get the stuff they left out there. Sasha has some makeup for you. Sorry I ruined the surprise."

My hands drop off his shoulders and my eyes fly to Belle's. She's holding her hands up to forestall my panic but I see fear in her own eyes.

"Skylar, I'm sure they're fine. Rex would have checked with AIRIA first to make sure the weather was safe. Not that I'm not going to kill my daughter for going out there without checking with me first but they're probably already back inside. We left our stuff just outside the doors, remember?"

She's right, I'm sure they're fine but the hairs on the back of my neck are raised and something is nagging at the back of my mind. Something that I heard but then forgot. It's right there on the edge of a memory but I can't quite grasp it. That is until AIRIA's voice floods the room and then it comes back to me.

Perimeter breach! Exterior door breach attempted! Oh My God! Someone tried to get in! Someone knows we are here!

"Rex Larson authorization level decreased from green to red."

Chapter Twenty-Three ... Rex

I stand back and study my reflection in the mirror while Matty and Ben blast space invaders on the TV behind me. I can't remember ever caring about how I looked before but I know the girls have been working on special outfits for the party tonight and I want to look good for Skylar. All I have to wear is the same jeans and canvas work shirt that everyone else has been wearing since we came inside but Belle's made all of us guys vests to go over the shirt to jazz it up some. I'm just happy she didn't have time to make matching ties to go with the vests. I do like the new haircut she gave me with the clippers. It's much better than the blunt cuts she used to give us all with dull scissors by candle light. I take one more look at my reflection and then shrug my shoulders and turn away.

The boys are as cleaned up as they're going to get and occupied with the video games they brought over from the other side. I look at the wall clock and see that there's still an hour and a half until dinner will be served and think about going to the kitchen to beg for a snack to tide me over. It's funny how before we came inside food was strictly rationed and I never thought about snacking but now that there's plenty, it seems like I'm always hungry. Maybe before, my body knew there wasn't food so it didn't ask and now it knows there's lots so it wants more.

I'm about to head out when Sasha steps into the room and I do a double take. She doesn't look the same. She looks…different…good different! Her hair's changed and it makes her look older, more like a young woman.

"Rex, there you are. I need a favor, for Skylar!"

I'm still trying to get over this different version of her so I just nod and she keeps on talking.

"We have new dresses and new hair but I wanted to give Skylar something special to say both I'm sorry and thank you. She's never used…uh, never mind. I just have some things that I'd like to give her to go with her outfit for tonight but I don't know how to get them."

I shrug, "Ok, where are they? I can help you track them down in a storage room."

She bites her lip uncertainly and glances at the boys but they're lost in their battle so she steps closer. "The stuff I want to give her is in our bags that we left outside. Do you think any of it would have survived the rain?"

Outside? Huh, I've got to think about that for a minute. We had all ran inside at the time and most of us hadn't brought anything with us. It's the first time I've thought about what we left out there. I look over at Matty and realize that I left something really important out there too. I've kept our Mom's wallet with everything that I thought was important in her purse with me all these years. The only thing Matty has of her are a few pictures that are in that wallet. I can see in my mind the backpack the wallet was in and where I left it in the tent. I have to get it for him. I focus back on Sasha after taking another quick look at the clock on the wall. There's time before the party starts to run out and get the things we want.

"I'm pretty sure our stuff should be ok. It was all under tarps and in the tents. Even with the damage the rain was doing to them, most of our things in the packs should have made it through. The biggest problem is, what's it like out there right now?"

Sasha's eyes look up at the speaker in the ceiling before looking back down at me with impatience. I find myself doing my own eye roll. Different hair, same girl!

"AIRIA, what's the weather like outside right now?"

"Rex Larson, current weather is scattered cloud cover but mainly sunny. Do you wish a long term forecast?"

"Uh, no thanks AIRIA."

Sasha gives me a double thumbs up. "Ok, great. Let's run out and grab that stuff right now. I want Skylar to have plenty of time to learn how to use it before the party and I know Mom's going to want time to put it on too!"

I give Sasha a confused look. "What exactly are you going to get out there?"

She gives her head an impatient shake sending soft red curls bouncing.

"That's a secret and you'll just have to wait until the party to see the final results. Can we go, please?"

Before I have time to say yes, I'm interrupted.

"I wanna go to! I've never been outside!"

Ben's on his knees facing backward over the back of the couch. His face is filled with excitement and I wince at having to dash his hopes but AIRIA beats me to it.

"Benjamin Ross, you are unauthorized to leave the interior of the cavern."

His face immediately turns to a pout. "That's not fair!"

I step over and ruffle his hair.

"Listen, buddy, going outside for your first time is a pretty big deal. Don't you want Skylar to be with you for that? I think she'd be really upset if she didn't get to see your face the first time you saw the sky. Hang tight little man, we'll all be going out there together very soon."

Ben's expression changes from pouty to disappointment but he slumps back down on the couch and picks his controller back up to play again so I turn away and wave Sasha out the door.

We're half way to the barracks exterior door when I stop and hesitate. I turn and look back the way we come and search the main area for Lance, Ethan or Marsh to let them know what we're doing, but I don't see any of them. Sasha gives my arm a yank to get me moving again but I stand firm and think about going to find one of them.

"Come on, Rex! Please, the party's going to start soon. This will only take a few minutes!"

Her words sway me and I start moving towards the door again. She's right, our camp wasn't more than forty feet from the main door and it'll only take a few minutes to get there, grab our packs and get back. We'll have to come back out another day and try and salvage the rest. I'm sure we aren't the only ones who left precious belongings outside when we escaped the rain.

When we reach the front of the barracks, Sasha marches right up to the main overhead door and waves at me to open it. I shake my head and grab her arm to redirect her to the smaller man-sized door beside it. I can just imagine the panic that would happen if the main door rolled up. I'd rather just get out and back without having to explain to too many people what we were doing. There'll be time for everyone to go out and get their belongings on a day when there isn't a party planned.

The small door slides open when I put my palm on the scanner and we step into the airlock. I don't know why but I'm starting to get a bad feeling about this. I chalk it up to the frantic race to safety we went through the last time I was outside but I reach out and snag a communicator from a shelf full of charging stations. There is a whole row of hooks along one wall with heavy winter gear hanging from them and I make Sasha put one on as well. Even with ARIA's assurances that the weather's safe, I can't go out there without some kind of protection. Seven years of deep freeze will stay with me for a long time.

When I palm open the next door, we both have to squint at the light that blasts through. I take a hesitant step over the threshold and stop there in amazement. The landscape is still a miserable grey wasteland - but the sky, the sky! Grey/black patchy clouds float against a sky so blue it hurts my eyes. There's a slight chill in the air but nothing like the bone-freezing temperatures we've lived with for so long and it doesn't stop the soft kiss of heat on the top of my head. I slowly turn and catch something in the corner of my eye but I can't help but lift my face and feel something I haven't felt in seven long years. The sun's rays wash over my face and I'm so thrilled I feel tears prick at my eyes.

I just want to stand there for hours and soak it up but Sasha nudges me to the side breaking the spell.

"Soon, soon we'll all get to live out here again, Rex, but today we're having a party so let's get what we came for and get back to our friends and family."

I suck back the emotion and step out of the way so the door will close behind us. Sasha and I start walking towards the area our camp had been and we can see piles of what was left spread out everywhere in the distance. I'm still preoccupied with thoughts of the sun and how Ben's not the only one who will need to come out here. Matty was just a baby when the sun went away. I doubt he remembers what it looked or felt like.

We're half way to the first of the camps remains when my feet slow down. What did I see? I slowly turn and look back the way we had come but this time I keep my eyes down on the ground instead of the sky. I slowly track back our footprints until my eyes reach the door then scan the side of the mountain. Something doesn't look right. Something's out of place. My eyes zero in on one area and I squint against the sun and distance to try and figure out what's bothering me until…my eyes go wide. There's a section of the fake rock missing from the main overhead door. It almost looks like someone pried it off and tried to open…Sasha!

I spin around and lunge in her direction but she's already reached the edge of the camp debris and movement from the right has my head turning to see two figures rush out from behind some of our half strung tarps and head straight at her.

"SASHA!"

Her head shoots up and half turns my way but stops when she sees the men rushing at her. She tries to backpedal but her feet get tangled in a dirty discarded blanket and she falls backward onto her butt. The men reach her first and one of them reaches down and hauls her to her feet. I slam to a stop a few feet away and we all stare at each other for a minute until the man holding Sasha's arm in a painful grip cracks a sneer and gives a hoot of triumph.

"Whoooo hoooo! Look at this Popper, we got two keys here to that big fancy door!"

I let my shoulders slump and shake my head. "Those doors will never open for you and even if they did, you're outnumbered."

The man called Popper bounced on his feet and gave a crazy laugh. "They always open the doors when we come round…for dinner!"

I have no idea what the guy's talking about so I look away to the one holding Sasha. He seems slightly saner and he proves that he is with his next words.

"They'll open alright, you'll tell us everything we need to know. It's hard to keep secrets when you see your own leg roasting on an open fire for dinner."

Sasha's skin turns even whiter and she starts to gag at the image this freak has painted for us but he just smiles like it's all a big joke. "Yup, you'll tell us how to open the doors and all our family will be here to see what kind of goodies are inside! Won't be outnumbered then!"

I swallow the fear building in my throat. He's right, at some point one of us will tell them what they want to know if they really do what they said they would. Matty, Ben, Skylar and all the others are safe inside. Right now the only way those doors will open from out here is if I ask AIRIA to open them. I slowly move my hand to the communicator on my belt and tap the screen. Popper sees the movement and dives for my arm but he's too late, the screen lights up.

"AIRIA, DECREASE MY AUTHORIZATION FROM GREEN TO RED!!!"

Her voice floats from my waist as Popper and I hit the ground together.

"Rex Larson, authorization decreased from green to red, goodbye."

My eyes lift up from the dirt and meet Sasha's horrified eyes. She knows what I just did means that now no one can open the doors from out here, no matter what they do to us.

Chapter Twenty-Four ... Skylar

"AIRIA, where is Rex and who lowered his authorization level to red?"

"Skylar Ross, Rex Larson is located outside the cavern. Rex Larson requested the authorization level change."

I shake my head and look at Belle.

"That doesn't make sense! Why would he do that? He can't get back inside without a green level." I turn my face upwards and ask,

"AIRIA, who is with Rex?"

"Skylar Ross, Sasha Coombs is with Rex Larson as well as two other unknown subjects."

I fire back right away. "As in, two other people from the barracks?"

"Skylar Ross, the two other unknown subjects have not been in the barracks. They penetrated the perimeter seventeen days ago. The subjects attempted to breach the barracks exterior door and failed."

My eyes bounce from Belle to Ben as my heart rate kicks up a notch and my breathing starts to come faster.

"I thought it was a dream. I was sick and I thought it was part of the dream! Rex, Rex is out there and Sasha! Oh, oh no! I've got go out there. I've got go get them! How did this happen? Oh God!"

I lunge past Ben and yank open the closet door. My holster and gun are in my hand in seconds and I start strapping it on. The rifle, I'll need the rifle too! I throw the sling over my shoulder and pivot on my heel. I have to save him. This can't be happening. I can't lose him again! I know what they'll do. They'll take his clothes and then shoot him in the back. I can't let that happen again! Ben needs his father, I'll save him!

"SKYLAR! Snap out of it!"

I'm trying to get to the door but something's in my way. Something's holding me back but I can push through. I can… "Ouch!" Belle? Did she just slap me?

"Skylar! I need you to **think**! You can't just race out there all alone in a dress and sandals. We need to get Lance and the others. You aren't going out there alone!"

I focus in on her face as her words penetrate the fog of panic in my brain. Her face is so pale it's like there's no blood left under her skin. Her daughter's out there in just as much danger as Rex, she must be so worried. I hear someone crying and look over to see my baby brother with tears pouring down his face. Oh, oh Ben, I almost left you all alone. I give my head a shake and pull away from Belle so I can kneel down in front of him. I pull him into my arms for a few seconds and then hold him away from me.

"Ben, calm down. It's going to be alright. Everything will be ok. I'm going to get them back! Do you believe me?"

He sniffs back his tears and slowly nods his head.

"You can do it, Sky. You always make everything better!" His little lips quiver on the last word so I give my head a sharp nod of agreement.

"That's right. It's my job to take care of things and I'm really good at my job!"

I pull him in for another quick hug before releasing him and pushing up to my feet.

"AIRIA, are they still inside the perimeter?"

"Skylar Ross, all four are moving southeast and will cross the boundary in four minutes."

"Can you track them?"

"Skylar Ross, affirmative. Rex Larson is in possession of a communication device."

"Ok, keep tracking them. Please alert Lance, Ethan, and Marsh that we need them over here. Tell them it's an urgent situation."

I look at Belle and see tears tracking down her face as she twists her hands into knots.

"We **will** get them back!"

When she nods back, I glance down at the yellow dress and shake my head.

"I'm just going to go change."

I race past her to my room and reach down to pull the yellow fabric up over my head but pause first and close my eyes. This dress, the dance, what was I thinking? There's just no room in this world for teenage girl fantasies. I let out my breath and with it all the dreams I thought I could have and then yank the gown over my head and drop it into a pile on the floor.

It only takes me minutes to change into my sturdy cargos and an undershirt with a flannel over it. I'm pulling on my boots over heavy socks when I hear the guys voices come into the other room. So I shove my last boot on and hit the door.

They're all talking at once as Belle tries to explain what we know so I just put two fingers into my mouth and let out a piercing whistle to bring silence. When all eyes are on me, I wave my arm for them to follow and head into the cavern. We can talk as we gear up.

"Rex and Sasha went outside for some reason. There were two unknown people out there waiting for them and they are now heading towards town. Rex changed his authorization level to red. I can only assume it was so they couldn't force him to open the door. He, he must have been trying to protect all of us. AIRIA's tracking them and now we're going to get them back!"

Lance grabs my arm just as I reach the shooting gallery and swings me around.

"We have to go. We can't let them get to town! If it's the monsters that moved in there from the ski resort, you just have no idea what we're facing. They are pure evil! We have to get to them before they reach the main group." Lance drops my arm and turns to go back while saying over his shoulder. "I'm going to get my bow!"

"Stop!" I yell at him. He spins back towards me with an impatient scowl. "You and Ethan were in the army, right?" When they both nod, I push open the door of the shooting gallery revealing the gun racks and all the weapons stored there behind glass.

"Then it's time to stop playing Robin Hood and get back to being soldiers!"

I step aside and let them enter the room while Belle and Marsh hold back at the door. "We aren't going to mess around with bows and arrows." I reach up to a shelf on the wall and pull down an old coffee cup. The keys to the cases are hidden inside so Ben wouldn't have access to them. I toss the keys to Lance and waved at the locked drawers underneath the glass. "Ammunition is down there. Bring lots! I'll meet you back here in a few."

I step out of the room and attempt to go around Belle and Marsh but she grabs my arm.

"Skylar, we have to hurry! They're getting further away with every minute."

Before I have a chance to reassure her, Marsh does.

"Don't worry, Belle. I'm sure Rex will drag his feet to keep them slowed down. We'll catch up to them by the time they hit pavement."

She nods uncertainly and turns back to me. "What type of weapon would you recommend for me?"

I'm impatient to get the rest of the gear I need but I'm distracted by her words and the brave little face of Ben that's listening to everything we say.

"Belle, I need you to stay here." She immediately starts to shake her head but I hold up my hand to stop her protests. "Listen to me! I will do everything I can to get your daughter back; I need you to keep MY family safe. If anything goes wrong and we don't make it back here then there will be two little boys left all alone with strangers. I can't focus if I'm worried about Benny. I need to know you'll be here to care for him if the worst happens!" Her face falls but she reaches down and pulls Ben close to her side before sadly nodding so I turn to Marsh but before I can even ask him to stay too he's throwing up his hands.

"Not happening! Rex is my brother. I won't stay behind!"

I go to challenge him but time's ticking by so I just give him a curt nod and step to the side so he can arm up and then I'm running. I've left my holster and rifle in the living quarters and we'll all need the winter gear in the airlock. I hit the door running and slide through sideways before it's even open all the way. Holster strapped on, rifle slung, extra ammunition bulging from my cargo pockets and I'm across the room and into the airlock. I stuff gloves and winter hats into the sleeves of four parkas before scooping up four communicators from their charging stations.

My arms are full so I dump all the gear on a small trolley cart sitting outside one of the storage rooms and dash in. I pull one GO bag from the shelf and turn to race out but spin back around. Dad's words are still guiding me after all these years.

"One is none and two is one."

It means that if you only have one item and it's lost or broken you have none but if you have two of the same things you have a backup and still have one. He used that rule with all the planning he did to stock our supplies.

I don't plan on us failing or being stuck outside for any length of time but plans have a way of falling apart so I pull three more bags off the shelf and dump them on top of the jackets on the trolley. I'm pushing it so fast across the cavern that I almost send the whole thing tipping over into the stream when I hit the bridge. I need to calm down, slow down. Panic is when mistakes are made.

When I reach the far end of the cavern, the men are just coming out of the shooting range with weapons strapped onto their bodies. I push the trolley up to the group and dump the GO bags at their feet before passing out jackets. As they shrug on the heavy winter gear, Lance prods one of the packs at his feet and starts shaking his head.

"Too heavy! If we have any chance of catching up to them then we need to go light and fast. This stuff will just slow us down."

I reach down and pull a pack up and onto my back and start walking towards the back right of the cavern.

"Bring them and follow me."

I ignore his objections and keep going until I come to another door. It slides open when I palm it and I reach up and take down a ring full of different keys. I can hear the others coming so I start pulling tarps off everything in the room and turn and wait for them to join me. When Lance steps in and gives a low whistle at what the room contains I again, toss him a set of keys.

"We aren't running. We're driving."

Chapter Twenty-Five ... Rex

I try and ignore Sasha's sobs and the burning rage that's a ball smoldering in my gut as these two animals push us down the trail. I try and keep my cool and be smart. I let my feet catch on every rock and root so that I do more stumbling than walking. Anything I can do to slow us down and give our people time to catch up with us will help.

I let the toe of my boot catch on a root and control my stumble into the man in front of me who keeps putting his hands on Sasha every chance he gets. We both tumble to the side of the trail but it has the desired result of removing his hands from her and delaying us a few more precious minutes. The cuff across the side of my face in payment for my clumsiness is worth it.

I keep my mouth shut and let the rage simmer. I'm almost as mad at ourselves as I am at these two freaks. We were so stupid and careless. Seven years of watching our backs and taking every precaution to stay safe and the minute we get a few comforts, it's all washed away with the hot water of our first shower.

Popper and his partner enjoyed telling us just how easy it was for their group to find us as they herd us forward with the threat of a very large hunting knife and one small handgun.

Once their gang had taken over the hotel and town, they had started scouting out the area and immediately saw the huge smoke clouds from all the fires our group had made to stay warm before Skylar had let us inside. It was only the luck of the rain that kept them from moving on us right away. We would have been sitting ducks if they had found us all out in the open. When there was a break in the weather, a group of them had come up the mountain to search for us but had only found what was left of the camp we abandoned when Skylar opened the door for us. None of us even thought about the trail of tracks over a hundred people would leave, leading straight into the side of a mountain wall.

It took them a few days to figure out but eventually, they started pulling off the false front of rock and then tried to break open the solid steel door. When the leader realized it wasn't going to open, he left these two to sit and wait for someone to come out.

"You two are going to be our can openers! HAW HAW HAW!"

Popper's laugh is the sound of a dying goose and it makes my teeth ache every time he let loose with it. Apparently, I'm not the only one bothered by it because his partner sticks a dirty finger in one ear and wiggles it around.

"Will you shut up with that stupid laugh, already? Man, I can't WAIT to get back to the hotel and get away from you! Seventeen days stuck with your dumb ass. What the hell did I do to Gail to deserve this punishment?"

"HAW HAW HAW, don't you remember? Last raid you only brought back that one skinny kid. He wasn't even enough for a snack for everyone! She was maaaad at you! HAW HAW HAW!"

I have to swallow hard to push the vomit back down at his words but Sasha loses it and starts to heave. She manages to turn to the side of the path and lean over before she throws up again and again.

I close my eyes and wait for her to finish as the sound of Popper's honking goes on and on. I know our people will get to us in time but after that, we need to exterminate every single one of these freaks. No one can even think about rebuilding a world with their type in it.

It doesn't take much longer after we get moving again before we stumble out of the dead trees and onto pavement. This is the road that will lead us into town and the rest of the gang, so I know that if the rescue is coming, it will have to be soon.

We've only walked about a hundred feet down the road when I catch the faint sound of engines. It's hard to tell but it sounds like a lot more than just one. I know Skylar has a truck so it's probably her and I don't want these idiots to have any warning so I start making noise.

"Hey, hey! Why are you guys doing this? With the weather finally clearing, we could start rebuilding. We could plant crops and grow as much food as we need! You don't need to resort to this kind of thing anymore! Everyone will have to come together to start fixing things!"

"HAW HAW HAW, who wants to work at that? This is way more fun! We get to do anything we want now and no one gets to say no!"

"Will you two SHUT UP! I can't even hear myself think with all your racket!"

Sasha thinks I'm actually trying to persuade these morons to work with us and finally finds her voice after spending the whole trip sobbing.

"No, no, it's true! You can join us. Back at the bunker, there's all kinds of…"

I jump in and cut her off before she can give them information I don't want them to have. I can't believe she'd be that dumb to tell these guys about what's inside.

"You shut up! You don't get to be a part of this conversation! It's all your fault we were outside to start with! Don't you say another word!"

I try and signal her with my eyes not to say anything else but her betrayal from before is still too fresh and she takes my words personally and starts to cry again. I blow out a frustrated breath but at least she's not telling them about the goldmine of supplies inside anymore.

Popper's partner gives me a shove to get me moving again and in the quiet I can no longer hear the sounds of engines. They must be coming the rest of the way on foot so I stay tense and ready for the moment when I'll grab Sasha and dive to the ground but we keep walking and nothing happens.

Thirty minutes later and I'm starting to freak out. We're almost to the edge of town and if these two join up with others in their gang then the rescue is going to get a lot harder. My head shoots up from the road disappearing under my feet when I catch the faint sound of voices ahead. We're on a curve in the road and as we come out of it I see a group of six men walking towards us. My whole body droops. Too late, eight men instead of two will be very dangerous.

When the group meets up with ours, I shuffle closer to Sasha and put an arm around her. We keep our heads down and try and stay on our feet as the new group pushes and pokes at us while making it clear exactly what's going to happen to us when we get into town. I clench my teeth and try not to look around desperately for the help I'm starting to think isn't coming. Sasha finally can't take anymore and she buries her face against my chest as she wails.

The men think this is hilarious but finally stop taunting us and instead push us down the road. We shuffle along as fast as we can with me practically supporting all of Sasha's weight and I try and listen to their conversation to get as much information as I can.

"You guys are lucky you caught some game! Jerod sent us to come bring you back to add to the menu. There's only three meals left in the pantry and Gail's starting to froth at the mouth! You know how nasty she gets when she's hungry so these two should calm her down a bit, especially if there's more where they came from."

Popper bounces around the group and lets out his god awful laugh.

"HAW, HAW, HAW, I'm too stringy for you guys to eat!"

There's a unanimous roar from the men. "SHUT UP!"

Popper's partner shakes his head. "Even if they tell us everything that's in their hideout, we might need a bomb to get that door open. I can't see the people inside just opening it up for us to raid."

One of the newcomers speaks up. "No problem! We found a couple of crates of dynamite at a construction site. We'll have that door open with one big BOOM!"

A shiver wracks my body as cold sweat runs down my back. I don't want to die and be a meal for these freaks but I'm ok with it if I know my family and friends will be safe. I'm pretty sure those bunker doors are meant to withstand a nuclear blast but I don't know for sure.

The road breaks out of the trees and onto an overpass so I've got a good view of the town below. Everything looks the same as the last time I was here but I don't want to think of the misery that awaits us. The overpass we stand on goes over the main highway that bisects the town. Standing here looking east, I can see quite a ways in the distance. Above are a few black and dark-grey clouds against the blue sky but far to the east covering the horizon is a solid line of blackness. It almost looks like dirty smoke but the wind is blowing in the wrong direction for me to smell anything.

Popper points towards the horizon and asks, "Is that a storm coming?"

One of the men shakes his head. "No moron, storms don't come from the east here. They come from the west or north! We don't know what it is but it started yesterday and it's growing and getting closer. Some of us think it's a wildfire."

The men don't really seem all that concerned as they shove us deeper into town and closer to the hotel they've taken over, but my eyes stay on the blackness. Something's coming and in this world we now live in, it's usually not good.

Chapter Twenty-Six ... Skylar

"On three, then heave. One, two, three!" Lance grunts out before heaving his end of the dead tree to the side of the road.

I grit my teeth to stop myself from screaming in frustrated rage. I left it up to Lance and Ethan to decide if they wanted to take my Dad's truck or the ATV's and they had chosen the truck. Lance wanted us to stay together and keep the engine noise to just one. Everything was fine until we made it half way down the overgrown track and came to the first downed tree across it. Six more trees blocked the way and Ethan guessed that the rain had weakened the soil enough for the dead trees to finally fall.

I turn my back to them and try and take a deep breath. The amazing feel of the sun on my face has lost its charm with how long this has taken. We all know we will never catch up with Rex and Sasha before they are taken into town. Our only hope is that they aren't killed right away because of the information the gang will want from them about the bunker. This rescue has now become much, much more dangerous. Even with all the firepower we've brought, we will still be greatly outnumbered and we'll have to go right into the lion's den to get our people back.

With the track finally cleared and the pavement in sight we all move to load back into the truck. Just as I'm about to open the truck door, I hear something out of place. I look at Marsh and see he's got his head cocked to the side with a frown.

"Do you hear that too?" I ask him. He looks over at Lance who starts nodding.

"Engines and more than one but not close by. They could be anywhere. Sound travels further now with no background noise. I didn't see any vehicles up at the resort when I scouted it out but they may have had some I didn't see. We're going to have to be very careful once we hit the main road." He gives us all a grim look. "Be ready to shoot if we run into any of them."

We keep the truck's windows down with our eyes and ears open but see nothing as we get closer to town. Just before we come to the end of the tree line and the overpass, Lance turns down a rutted overgrown siding and edges the truck in under the trees as far as he can. We spread a grey tarp over it and pile as much brush as we can find overtop of it. From here on out, we go by foot.

We stay off the roads and parallel the town inside the tree line until we start to hear noises. Using the binoculars from the Go bags we all crawl right to the edge of the trees and scan the buildings in front of us. I haven't been in this town since my Dad drove us through the day the bombs dropped but the others have lived here for the last seven years and know what they're looking for.

"Looks like they took over the hotel and made it their base," Lance grunts out.

I scan the buildings until I see an old faded sign for what used to be a higher end hotel. The parking lot has been cleared of cars and they used them to form a crappy barricade along the perimeter of the property. It's not going to stop anyone on foot from going over and that's exactly what we are going to do because being shoved across the parking lot, past a blazing bonfire is Rex and Sasha. My eyes follow them to one corner where they're pushed into the back of a cargo van. When the overhead door slams down, I can't help but track back to the oily smoke floating up over the fire and to the "thing" that's being turned slowly on a spit over it. When I get a clear look at exactly what is being cooked I drop my binoculars to the ground, lurch backward on my hands and knees until I can't control it anymore. The hot acidic vomit sprays out of me while rage fills me and tears slide down my face.

When my body stops heaving and I catch my breath, I wipe my mouth with the sleeve of my jacket and turn to see that the other guys have pulled back too. I meet each one of their gazes and feel my expression harden.

"We are going to kill them all!"

No one disagrees with me. We pull back from the tree line and discuss our options. The only real plan we can come up with is to wait for dark, create a distraction and then sneak in and try to free Rex and Sasha. The main thing we all agree on is to kill as many of them as we can while we're at it.

Lance draws a rough outline of the hotel and grounds with both Ethan and Marsh filling in details. He taps on one section of the map.

"This is the generator room. We know Ted was abandoning ship because there wasn't any gas left to pump the water, but these guys must have gas or they wouldn't have set up shop here. It would be too far to haul water for that many people. If we can get into that room and cause it to blow up or start a fire, they should all come running."

Marsh makes a humming noise in his throat and shakes his head.

"No way, that's under the main lobby. There's going to be way too much activity in that area to sneak in and then out undetected and it's pretty close to where they put Rex and Sasha." He taps on a different area of the map. "No one but us was using this wing of the hotel so most likely the gang would have settled in the area where the rooms were already set up from before. There's a better chance of that wing still being empty. Ted pulled a lot of our supplies from our rooms after he kidnapped Ethan and Belle, but there was still a lot left when I was sneaking around before we all evacuated for the mountain. All the batteries and some of the gas cans were still in the janitor's closet we used for our storage. If these guys haven't found them yet we can use that stuff to set the wing on fire. It'll pull people further away from the front and we have a better chance of getting in and out without getting caught."

Lance rubs his chin and nods. "Yeah, I like that better. As long as the fire is big enough, all eyes will be on it or they'll be racing inside to pull out and save whatever supplies they have in the main hotel. Once it gets dark enough, we'll all move up and find cover at the back of the hotel. Marsh, you and I will go in and start the fire. Ethan, you and Skylar will stay outside and make sure no one decides to come into that wing from outside. Once the fire's set, we all meet back up and circle around to the side the kids are being kept. Two things worry me though; one - getting the cargo van door open, it looked like they put a padlock on it and two - we have no way of knowing if there are people living in that wing. We could be walking into a hornet's nest completely outnumbered. If we start firing our weapons the element of surprise goes right out the window."

I lean over the drawing and make a curved arrow with my finger. "If we come around this area we would be at the end of the wing we need to get into. It would give us a better view of both side's windows. We'd have to wait until it's dark but anyone in there would have some kind of light source we could see from the outside. No light, plan's a go. If there are lights, we think of something else. What's on that side of the hotel we could use for cover while we wait for it to get dark?"

The others lean back and think about the area around that wing before Ethan answers. "I remember there was a fast food restaurant and a gas station on that side but that's it for me. Marsh?"

His son points to the area on the drawing. "Yup, burger shack, gas and go and then offices. Across from that is a strip mall with a ski rental place, hair salon and I think a real estate office."

Lance nods. "Ok, we go to the strip mall for the best view." He glances up and looks at the setting sun and I follow his look.

This is the first sunset I've seen in seven years. It should be momentous but the danger we are about to walk into makes me think it also might be the last one I ever see.

"We should go now and start circling around to the other side. We need to get this done early enough that they aren't inside getting ready for bed. The more of them out in the courtyard we can see the better. After they go in, anyone can just look out those windows and see us. We wouldn't even know we've been spotted. It'll also mean more of them distracted by the fire. Let's get back to the truck and dump our bags. The faster we can move the better and the bags will just slow us down."

We reach the truck quickly and pull what we need from them before leaving our bags in the bed. I spot the tool box and remember Lance's other concern. He sports a grin when he pulls a pair of bolt cutters from the box. Goodbye padlock!

I try and stay focused as I follow Lance and Marsh, with Ethan behind me bringing up the rear, but my mind won't stop thinking. There's a very good possibility that I won't make it back up the mountain tonight. This isn't a TV show or a movie where the good guys always win. This is real life and in this life, a lot of people have died and are still dying. I know Belle will watch over Ben and keep him safe inside but it breaks my heart that I might not be around to see him grow up into a man.

We make it to the back of the strip mall without being seen and as soon as the sun dips behind the mountains in the west we slink around the side and slip into the middle business that was once a hair salon. There's still a faint smell of hair chemicals and perfume in the air and when I see the row of stylist chairs in front of shattered mirrors, I raise my hand and touch my hair. It's completely surreal to me that a few hours ago I was having my own hair styled for the first time in my life and now I'm getting ready to kill a bunch of strangers. My fingers find the yellow ribbons that are still weaved into the waves of my hair. As we hunker down and wait for full dark, I can't help but smirk. If I die tonight, I'll die with kickass hair!

Chapter Twenty-Seven ... Rex

The biggest shock I get when we are pushed through the crowd in front of the hotel is the way these people look. I was expecting maniac psychopaths with crazy tattoos and piercings. Instead, they all just look like normal people. Dirty, oily, smelly people with major dental issues but still just normal people. A few in the crowd cheer and taunt us but most just stare with blank looks as we are shoved past. I try and meet every gaze to see if there's anyone here who might regret their choices and help us. The best I get is a few who drop their eyes and turn away. We're on our own unless someone comes to rescue us.

We get pushed through the main doors into the dim lobby and I scan around to see what's changed since I was last here. Except for a few piles of boxes and bins, it's the same. Right down to the hopeless worn down expressions on the new residents. We get led through the corridors and up a few flights of stairs until we come to a set of double doors. A brisk knock has them opening and when we step through I see a fancier version of all the other hotel rooms I've been in.

There are two people lounging on a couch and I'm amazed when the woman stands and greets us with a smile. I take a quick look at Sasha to see if she's seeing the same thing as me and her expression tells me she is. This woman is absolutely gorgeous and she looks like she's just stepped off of a fashion runway. Her long black hair shines and bounces with health and cleanliness. Expertly applied makeup makes her face glow and her lipstick perfectly matches the rose coloured silk dress she's wearing paired with high heels. I can't remember ever seeing someone who looks this perfect even before the bombs dropped.

The other person in the room is a man who looks just as clean and put together but he stays seated and studies us with hard eyes. I flinch when the woman gets close enough to me to reach out and take my chin between two fingers that have shiny nail polish on them. Her green eyes sparkle with amusement at my flinch and she murmurs in a cultivated voice, "So young. So handsome!"

I wrench my face from her grasp and try and step back but one of our guards shoves me back into place. The woman's laugh comes out like a child's and she claps her hands in glee.

"I LOVE young!"

Her gaze leaves me and she turns to Sasha where her expression changes from glee to admiration.

"Oh my! Will you look at that gorgeous hair! I've always wanted to be a redhead and that pale creamy skin, so…delicious!"

Sasha chokes out a sob at the last word and tries to move closer to me but is held firmly in place by another guard.

"Stop messing with them, Gail." The man on the couch says before pushing to his feet and addressing the men holding us.

"Where'd you find them?"

Popper slides around from behind the guards and launches into his routine.

"HAW, HAW, HAW, we got em Jerod! Me and Malcolm, just like you told us too. We waited *forever* but the can finally opened and out came these treats!"

Jerod shakes his head in annoyance but the woman, Gail's face transforms into a scowl of disgust and disdain, showing the lines and wrinkles of wear that she's hiding under her mask of cosmetics.

Jerod points an angry sharp finger at Popper and orders, "Out!"

"HAW, HAW, HAW, sure, sure boss!" Before he skitters back around us and out of the door. Malcolm takes his place and holds out his hand to Jerod. Resting on his palm is the communicator he took from me.

"The boy was wearing it when we grabbed him. He talked into it and it answered him."

Jerod's eyebrows shoot up in surprise and he takes it from Malcolm and turns it over in his hands until he touches the screen and it lights up.

"Ooooh, pretty! What's it do?" asks Gail while leaning over his shoulder.

Malcolm shrugs, "Nothing since I took it from him. It'll light up but that's all. You'll have to persuade the kid to explain it."

Jerod gives me a penetrating look. “This is a fancy piece of tech to still be working when everything else died years ago. Do you want to tell me what it does?”

I just shake my head “no”. I’m not telling these people anything.

He smirks knowingly and looks back down at the communicator in his hand.

“I wonder what else you’ve got hiding behind that big steel door. You both look well fed and clean so I’ll assume you have food and water but what else?” Sasha and I stay silent so he looks up at us and raises his eyebrows as if waiting for a reply and when we still don’t speak, a grin splits his face. “I think you have a lot behind that door and I think it will soon belong to me!”

Before he has a chance to say anything else, Gail interrupts him.

“Yes, yes, beating, starving, torturing and blah, blah, blah! Your fun will have to wait, darling. Did you forget? We’re hosting a dinner party tonight and we must make ourselves more presentable!” she sang in a sing-song voice while patting at her hair. “Whatever am I going to do with this hair? I’ll need the stylist sent up!”

Jerod glances away from us to Gail before rubbing wearily at his eyes.

“Gail, sweetheart, we’ve talked about this. No one’s coming for a party.”

The transformation that overcomes Gail has everyone in the room taking a half step back. Her perfect face cracks into one of rage showing every bit of the damage the last seven years has caused on her once beautiful face. She grabs two handfuls of her skirt material and rips at it while screaming.

“I will not be embarrassed by you in front of our guests! I need time to look my best before they arrive!”

Jerod holds up his hands in a calming movement. “Of course, of course, darling. But I don’t know how you could improve upon perfection!”

I'm completely floored by the switches in this woman and her next words confirm to me that she's bat guano crazy. Her face reverts to perfection and a blush even colours her cheeks.

"Oh Jerod, you're such a sweet talker! But I need a new dress! Whatever am I going to wear? Be a doll and have the boutique send over a few samples for me to choose from while my hair is being styled, pretty please." She bats her fake eyelashes at him before spinning on her heel and leaving the room.

Everyone is frozen in place at her display of insanity until the door closes behind her and then Jerod slowly turns towards us. For a fraction of a second, I feel sorry for this man when I see the pain in his eyes. He must really love the woman she once was and be broken by what she's turned into but then I remember what was being cooked in the fire outside and all traces of sympathy are washed away.

He waves us away with a weary dismissive half wave of his arm. "Put them in the pantry for now. I'll deal with them later."

As we get shoved back down the way we came in I hear one of our guards mutter under his breath.

"What a nutter!"

I try and start up a conversation with the guy but he just slams me between the shoulder blades with his rifle causing me to almost fall down the stairs we're descending. I try and wrack my brain for a way to use Gail's insanity to our benefit but all I can really think about is what's going to happen to us next.

When we reach the front lobby doors and emerge into the courtyard, I gag at overpowering the smell of roasting meat. I'm so disgusted when my mouth fills with saliva that I spit it out on the pavement in front of me, causing one of the guards to bark out a grim laugh and give me another shove.

"Don't sweat it, kid. You get used to it or well, I guess you won't be around long enough to."

I ignore the man and spit again. I wish Sasha would get it together a bit. She's pretty much done nothing except cry since we were captured. I know she's just a kid and we've kept her mostly away from what life's like since the bombs dropped, but I'm going to need her help if I can come up with an escape plan.

I'm pulled to a stop when we reach a large white cargo van and I watch closely as the guard uses a key that's on a string around his neck to open a padlock. When the door is rolled up, a different smell waffles out. It's one of human waste and rot and I've got no control over the instant gag reflex that overcomes me. This time the blow is against my head when I empty the contents of my stomach on the guard's boots.

I'm still reeling from the hit when I'm half lifted, half pushed up into the back of the van. My ears are ringing and Sasha has amped up her crying to wailing making it even worse. Once my head clears, I'm surprised that I can see my surroundings. I look up to find the light source and see that long four inch high slits have been roughly cut into the metal all the way around the ceiling. The lowering sun is shining directly into one side of the truck giving plenty of light. I guess they don't want their food stock suffocating.

When I go to push myself up to my feet, my hand lands on a rancid damp blanket that's no better than a shredded rag. I wipe my sticky hand off on my pants and try not to think about what's on it. Sasha sits on her knees with her arms wrapped around her head while she rocks herself back and forth with every wail. I crouch back down beside her and pull her against me.

"Stop, stop, Sasha! I've got you. It's going to be ok. Come on, take a deep breath. We're going to get out of here. I promise!"

Her wailing slows to down to a soft whimper as I rub her back and as I wait for her to calm down I scan the interior of the cargo area over her head. My eyes meet another's and I realize that we aren't alone in here. The man staring back at me is covered in filth but I think I've seen him before. In his arms is a woman that I'm not sure is even alive. Her eyes are so blank that it's not until she moves slightly that I see she's just in deep shock.

He nods his head slightly at me. "There's no way out, son. We've been here for five days and my son and I tried everything before they…took him."

His voice prompts my memory of where I know him from. He, his wife and adult son had been living in the basement of the town's recreation center and my group had done some trading with them over the years. They had a decent set up with gardens growing along the pool's edges. Belle would exchange clippings and sprouts with them to expand both of our varieties of vegetables that we grew.

"Mr. Chapman? Is that you?" At his startled look, I remind him of who I am. "My group use to trade with your family! Ethan, the doctor, treated your son when he got that gash in his leg infected. Belle and your wife use to exchange seeds for our gardens. Don't you remember me?"

He doesn't nod, just looks even sadder and leans over to kiss the top of his wife's head before speaking.

"You were good people, people we could trust. Did the rest of your group get caught by these animals too?"

I shake my head. "No, just Sasha and I so I'm hoping they'll be on the way to get us out of here! We have a safe place to go so your family can come with us when we get free."

His expression is so empty it hurts to look at and his next words are heartbreaking.

"Thank you for the offer young man but we won't be leaving here alive. They took our son and we know what they did to him. Neither of us wants to live in a world like that. We fought hard for years to stay alive. Now, we just want to be with our son." He looks away from me and rests his head on top of his wife's before gently lowering her limp body down to the bed of the van. It's when he slides down next to her and takes her limp hand in his that I see what they've done and understand. They both have jagged rips across their wrists and the blood that flows out of them is just a trickle as their lives slip away.

I have to look away as they take their final breaths and the roar of rage and helplessness fills my chest. To have fought so long and finally see the world start to heal only for their lives to end like this makes me furious. As I smother the scream in my throat and pull Sasha closer, I make a vow. We will survive this and when we get free, I will do everything possible to destroy every single one of these monsters!

Chapter Twenty-Eight ... Skylar

I feel like throwing up with the ball of nerves in my stomach as I watch for Lance and Marsh to come back out of the door that they entered ten minutes ago. It feels like it's been an hour since they slipped into the hotel and every minute is agonizing.

We had all breathed a sigh of relief when full dark fell and no lights could be seen in the wing where we wanted to start the fire. I find myself chanting "Come on. Come on." Until Ethan silences me with a hand on my arm. A quick look at his drawn face shows me he's just as anxious as me for his family to get out of there safely.

A flicker catches my attention in one of the windows and it's soon followed by others as window after window shows flames shining behind the glass. I tear my gaze from the fires and zero back in on the exit door, praying it'll pop open any second but nothing happens. My legs are trembling and I'm about to stand up from my crouched position to run out of the hair salon, across the street to look for them when it finally happens. The door opens and slams back against the brick wall as Lance and Marsh come flying out.

Lance has an arm around Marsh's waist and he's half supporting him as they cross the parking lot and then the street. I hear Ethan suck in a breath when they get close enough for us to see Marsh's face. He has a waterfall of blood pouring out of a cut above one eye that's making half his face look solid red. Ethan's already pulling the small med kit he brought with us out of his pocket. He insisted on having it in case Rex or Sasha needed patching up. Now he'll be using it on his son instead.

I rush to hold the glass door open and Marsh drops to the floor as soon as they make it inside. Ethan's mopping his face with gauze in seconds.

"What happened? Is he injured anywhere else?" he asks while he works.

Lance drops down beside him and shakes his head before chugging back half a canteen of water. Marsh must not be too injured because he reaches over and snatches it from him. He pushes Ethan's hands away for a minute while he drains the rest of it. The minute it comes down from his lips, Ethan's back at work.

"This needs stitches but it's a straight clean cut. Knife?"

Lance leans over and peers at the wound for a second before settling back.

"Yeah, there was a couple we surprised in one of the rooms. He got a swing at Marsh before I was able to take him down."

Before he can say anything else, we're all jolted by the sound of cracking and popping as the windows start to burst out from the spreading fires. Lance turns away from the window and pulls a flashlight out and shines it on his son's face.

"You good to go? We need to make our move."

Marsh tries to nod but Ethan hisses at him to stay still as he adds another butterfly bandage to the four he's already put on to seal the cut for now. Stitches will have to wait. Ethan does one more swipe with an alcohol wipe to clear as much blood from Marsh's face as he can before stuffing the contents back into the kit and jamming it back into his pocket.

"Skylar, Sky…Hey SKYLAR!"

I can't stop staring at the blood that's stained all down Marsh's throat and jacket but his harsh tone snaps me out of it and I tear my eyes from it and meet his.

"I asked if you're ready to go! Seriously, are you up for this because Rex and Sasha need us now?"

"Yes! Of course, we should get moving. All eyes should be on the fire by now."

He stares at me hard for another second before nodding and pushing to his feet. He's right, I need to be ready for what comes next. We all might end up bloodied by the time this night's over and freezing up isn't an option if we want to succeed. I need to keep it together.

We slip out of the back door of the salon and use the abandoned buildings for cover as we make our way to down the street closer to the front of the hotel across from where Rex and Sasha are being held. We line up behind Lance as he peeks around the corner of a sandwich shop that's directly across the street from the front lobby of the hotel. Again, it feels like we're waiting forever before he gives the signal for us to run across the street. I try and keep my eyes ahead of me to the car barricade we are running to but I can't help but look over at the wing that's being devoured by fire. There's plenty of people over in that direction and the light from the fire shows a lot of them standing around watching it but also many that are treating it like a bonfire dance. As we hit a smashed up minivan and crouch down behind it, I wonder if these idiots get that the fire's not going to just stay in that wing. It won't be long before it moves to the main hotel that they've all been calling home.

We rest for a few minutes while Lance moves up and down the line of cars, scouting what's between us and the cargo van our people are in. I crouch down even lower when I hear shouting and the sound of running footsteps. As soon as they fade, Lance is waving us forward.

Climbing over the hoods of a few cars only takes seconds and we are in the courtyard. The fire has provided plenty of light to show us that there's no one between us and the van. Lance has told us it's best to walk quickly rather than run so we might pass as part of the gang, but it's almost impossible for me not to bolt as fast as I can to where I know Rex is waiting.

There's a layer of cold sweat covering my body when we make it to the van. Ethan, Marsh and I turn our backs to it and hold our weapons ready in case anyone comes near while Lance goes to work on cutting off the padlock. All I want to do is spin around to see if he's ok when I hear the door being rolled up but I keep my eyes scanning in every direction for any possible threat.

"Rex, Sasha come on. We've got move quickly!" I hear Lance say in a low voice before I hear two sets of feet hit the ground.

"I knew you'd come for us!" Rex says behind my back.

"Of course we did! Now let's get…"

Lance doesn't get to finish his sentence because just then the lobby doors are thrown open and out runs a group of six people. Four of them have rifles and they are already pointed at us. The other two are a very well dressed couple. The man has a handgun in one hand and a roller suitcase in the other. It only takes him a split second to have it pointed at us as well. The woman has a fur coat thrown over one arm and is chattering away like we aren't even here.

"Jerod, be sure to tip the bell boy so he doesn't damage my luggage! Last time there was a terrible scuff on one!"

My shock at her oblivious words doesn't distract me from aiming my rifle right back at them.

Four rifles pointed at four rifles and a handgun - stalemate. Everyone's frozen for a minute until Marsh throws out, "Well, this is a big bucket of suck isn't it?"

The man with the handgun looks us all over closely before nodding.

"So, came to get your friends did you? That works in my favour. We were just about to take our leave from this sad, rundown establishment and relocate to your area. Why don't you all lead the way?"

I can see Lance step between me and Marsh out of the corner of my eye and his expression is hard.

"Do you honestly think we'd let you anywhere near the rest of our people?" He asks while nudging me to move slightly to the side. I get what he wants and the others must too because we all take a step sideways so we aren't so close to each other.

This is going to be a shootout and most of us aren't going to make it out of here alive. The thought is strangely calming to me. Ben's safe and he's got people to take care of him. If I've got to die, at least it will be while ridding the world of this filth.

My finger comes away from the guard and settles on the trigger. I'm ready for what comes next…until I'm not.

Red fireflies start dancing in front of me until each of the people pointing weapons at us has one centered on their chests. I know what they are but my brain's slow to put the pieces together so I risk turning my head to look at the others. Lance, Marsh, and Ethan are in my line of site and I see the same red light on them as well. My head moves in slow motion as I drop my chin and look down. There in the center of my own chest is a solid red light and that's when my brain catches up. Laser sights. We are being targeted! My head snaps up and starts scanning for where it's coming from when a loud screech of feedback followed by a booming voice blasts into the night.

"LOWER YOUR WEAPONS IMMEDIATELY! YOU ARE SURROUNDED AND SHOOT TO KILL ORDERS HAVE BEEN GIVEN FOR ANYONE NOT COMPLYING!"

Confusion and fear surge up inside me but at the same time, a vague sense of comfort also comes over me. I don't know what the frack is going on so I turn to look at Lance. He's as pale as I've ever seen him but I follow his lead as he slowly starts lowering his rifle to the ground. I see the others in my group doing the same but I keep my finger on the trigger because none of the gang are lowering theirs.

All my people are crouched down when the leader, Jerod, starts pointing his gun all around him and shouting into the night.

"Who the hell are you? Show yourselves!"

His answer is swift as gunfire shatters the night. All of us dive to the ground and stay there as bullet after bullet tears through the people facing us. My hand leaves the rifle to grope at my waist for my communicator. I bring it up in front of my face which is inches from the pavement and tap the screen to light it up. If AIRIA has any satellites in range then maybe she can tell me how many people are surrounding us and if we have any shot of getting out of here.

"AIRIA? AIRIA, I need help!"

I repeat her name again and again but there's no response. I'm so distracted by getting an answer from her that I don't even realize that the gunfire has stopped until hands grab the back of my jacket and haul me to my feet.

The communicator is ripped from my hands and I follow it with my eyes as it's passed to someone who's just walked up.

"I'm sorry, Skylar. AIRIA is no longer under your control. She belongs to me now."

The words hit me like a Mack truck. No, no that's not possible. AIRIA's mine! She's my mom and my dad and all I have left of them. No one can ***take*** her from me! Who the frack does this guy think he is?

I lift my eyes from the unresponsive communicator in his hands up to his face and stagger back a step.

"Uncle Bill?"

He's older and his face is harder than I remember, but it's him.

He gives a sharp nod. "Hello, Skylar. I was sorry to hear that your father is no longer with us. He would understand what will happen now. I've brought my people to take back what I loaned him so long ago. AIRIA is now under my complete control. Your authorization has been reduced to a red level but you don't have to worry, I will continue to shelter you for the sake of my friendship with your father. You just won't have any more authority in my bunker."

I should be happy to have a small part of my family show up but I don't know this man. All I know is that he's just taken away the only real parent I have left.

Coming Soon....

Sun & Smoke, Book Three in the Endless Winter series.

For more information, to leave a comment or sign up for a new release newsletter please visit:

www.theresashaver.com

Now Available: Frozen

A Stranded Novel

In January and February, normal nighttime temperatures in Alberta, Canada range from -15 to -25 °C (5 to -13 °F)

Winter temperatures can drop as low as -30 to -40 °C (-22 to -40 °F) for days at a time.

Although cold, these temperatures are manageable in modern civilization.

The odds of survival at these temperatures decrease when all modern conveniences such as furnaces and electricity are taken out of the equation. Such is the life many would face after an EMP.

Mrs. Moore's students had faced seeming insurmountable odds in getting home when they split up and traveled through a collapsing nation by Land and by Sea. Some of them didn't make it. Those that did found the sanctuary of Home overrun by gang members that had captured their friends and families and forced them into slave labour.

The students then did the unimaginable. They fought to free their town.

They won.

Teenagers forced to act well beyond their years to survive and tempered by the experience.

Parents - grateful to have them back but struggling to accept the changes in their children, attempt to force them back into the young roles they had before the end of civilization. What they don't realize is that it's not possible to erase those changes.

When the town is hit with a devastating virus, the teens once again take it upon themselves to rescue the town and find the medicine their loved ones so desperately need. Stonewalled at every turn they make the hard decision to embark on an epic journey to a faraway city to search the ruins for help they need.

Traveling through a Frozen wasteland, they not only have to battle the elements and other survivors but also the inner struggles of growing up too fast and coming to terms with the things they do.

It's not just the weather that has Frozen.

Also by Theresa Shaver

The Stranded Series

Land - A Stranded Novel
Sea - A Stranded Novel
Home - A Stranded Novel
City Escape - A Stranded Novel
Frozen - A Stranded Novel

Endless Winter Series

Snow & Ash
Rain & Ruin
Coming Soon - Sun & Smoke

To see descriptions or to get started on another book, please visit:

http://www.theresashaver.com/books.html

Made in the USA
Lexington, KY
04 August 2017